SHADOW SQUADRON

CRITICAL STRIKE

WRITTEN BY
CARL BOWEN

ILLUSTRATED BY
WILSON TORTOSA

COLORED BY
BENNY FUENTES

D1435687

2013.671

CAPSTONE
YOUNG READERS

INTEL

ZO19.681

Shadow Squadron is published by
Capstone Young Readers
A Capstone Imprint
1710 Roe Crest Drive
North Mankato, MN 56003
www.capstoneyoungreaders.com

Cataloging-in-Publication Data is
available on the Library of Congress
website.

ISBN: 978-1-62370-109-3 (paperback)

Summary: In the modern world of politics
and warfare, the critical battles take
place behind the scenes--and that's just
where Shadow Squadron excels.

Designed by Brann Garvey
Edited by Sean Tulien

Printed in China by Nordica
0414/CAZ1400599
032014   008120NORDF14

CONTENTS

1316.981

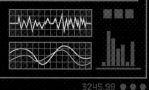

3245.98 ● ● ●

2012.101

ACCESS GRANTED

SHADOW SQUADRON

CROSS, RYAN

RANK: Lieutenant Commander
BRANCH: Navy SEAL
PSYCH PROFILE: Cross is the team leader of Shadow Squadron. Control oriented and loyal, Cross insisted on hand-picking each member of his squad.

WALKER, ALONSO

RANK: Chief Petty Officer
BRANCH: Navy SEAL
PSYCH PROFILE: Walker is Shadow Squadron's second-in-command. His combat experience, skepticism, and distrustful nature make him a good counter-balance to Cross's leadership.

YAMASHITA, KIMIYO

RANK: Lieutenant
BRANCH: Army Ranger
PSYCH PROFILE: The team's sniper is an expert marksman and a true stoic. It seems his emotions are as steady as his trigger finger.

BRIGHTON, EDGAR

RANK: Staff Sergeant
BRANCH: Air Force Combat Controller
PSYCH PROFILE: The team's technician and close-quarters-combat specialist is popular with his squadmates but often agitates his commanding officers.

JANNATI, ARAM

PHOTO NOT AVAILABLE

RANK: Second Lieutenant
BRANCH: Army Ranger
PSYCH PROFILE: Jannati serves as the team's linguist. His sharp eyes serve him well as a spotter, and he's usually paired with Yamashita on overwatch.

SHEPHERD, MARK

PHOTO NOT AVAILABLE

RANK: Lieutenant
BRANCH: Army (Green Beret)
PSYCH PROFILE: The heavy-weapons expert of the group, Shepherd's love of combat borders on unhealthy.

2019.681

MISSION BRIEFING

OPERATION

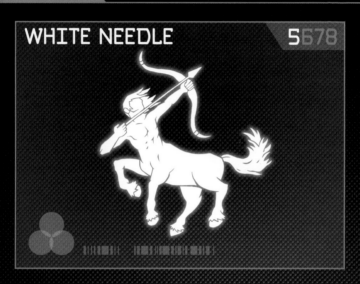

WHITE NEEDLE

5678

Syrian rebels have acquired a White Needle, or stolen chemical weapon. We already know they plan to use it, so it's our job to determine the target and prevent the launch. Two Israeli intelligence agents are willing to provide intel on the missing weapon in exchange for extraction from Syria. I'll be leading a team to rendezvous with them.

If we fail, gentlemen, it's likely that thousands of lives will be lost. I know we have the talent and technology to prevent that from happening. Let's get to it.

— Lieutenant Commander Ryan Cross

3245.98

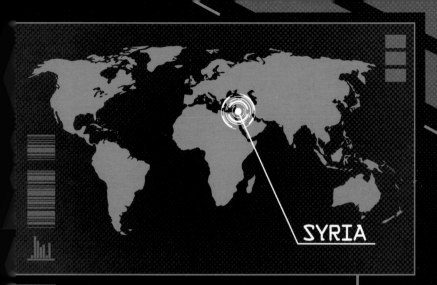

SYRIA

PRIMARY OBJECTIVE

- Rendezvous with Israeli forces
- Recover missing chemical weapon

SECONDARY OBJECTIVES

- Capture Syrian rebels responsible
- Limit enemy casualties

1932.789

0412.981

1624.054

1324.014

WHITE NEEDLE

Lieutenant Commander Ryan Cross led his four-man fireteam through the city of Al-Haffah, Syria. The center of the town lay ghostly and deserted. In the pale moonlight, the city's half-destroyed buildings loomed overhead like twisted fingers of dead giants trying to claw their way out from the earth.

"Lots of sniper holes, Commander," Lieutenant Kimiyo Yamashita warned Cross.

Yamashita was an experienced Army Ranger and the team's sniper, so Cross was inclined to take his word. Cross nodded. He directed the men to follow him closer to the cover of a ruined building nearby. The town had been shelled by the Syrian army's artillery at the command of President Bashar Al-Assad. He hoped to eradicate a group of rebels of the Free Syrian Army who had taken refuge there.

It was true that the overpowered rebels had fled to Turkey after the attacks, but Al-Haffah's battered landscape hardly

looked like victory. To Cross, the ruins suggested that Syria's president cared more about crushing the rebellion than he did protecting his people.

The rebels of the Free Syrian Army would probably agree with Cross's opinion. In late 2010, much of Syria's citizenry had carried out civil protests regarding the abuse of power by their government. The Syrian government responded violently to the protests, resulting in a civil war. While the United States, the United Nations, and other foreign entities would generally prefer to avoid interfering in civil conflict, President Assad's crackdown on rebels had been so brutal that the world couldn't stand by and do nothing.

The United States formally acknowledged the rebels' Free Syrian Army (or FSA) as the true voice of the Syrian people. Nations on every border of Syria took in refugees who fled from the violence. A few allowed FSA rebels to hide on their soil while they regrouped and readied for the next battle.

For its part, the US considered itself invested in Syria's future. It had every reason to hope that the FSA would topple President Assad's ruthless regime. Hopefully, the Syrian government that arose from a rebel victory would take better care of its people's needs.

Aside from publicly voicing its support, the US government had taken no action to aid the rebels against their government. No weapons were donated, and no troops were deployed. To most of the world, America had taken no steps whatsoever.

Officially.

Unofficially, however, America involved itself in the Syrian conflict in one major way: It deployed Ryan Cross's Shadow Squadron.

Cross signaled toward a bombed-out house not far from the objective. "Take position there and get ready to give us some cover," Cross said to Yamashita, his voice barely a whisper. "Just in case we need it."

"Sir," Yamashita said.

Shadow Squadron was a top-secret unit comprised of elite soldiers from all branches of the military. It attracted only the best of the nation's soldiers and employed them on ultra-sensitive, top-secret missions — even missions they couldn't officially (or legally) be involved in. Therefore, while the US government claimed to have no official presence in Syria, it did have its best men on site to keep an eye on things.

The main US concern was that Syria's government possessed vast stockpiles of chemical weapons. The Syrian government had even begun moving them within the country as if they were preparing to use them.

If the government collapsed and the rebels weren't able to restore order quickly enough, there was a real concern that some of the chemical warheads would fall into the wrong hands. Terrorists, criminals — any madman among them could cause destruction and chaos with those weapons.

Complicating things even further, certain terrorist organizations had taken an interest in helping the FSA against President Assad's government. Al-Nusra Front, or the Front for

Victory of the People of Syria, had been committing reckless bombings and paramilitary attacks against the Syrian army since the beginning of 2012. Most of the FSA disapproved of their extreme tactics.

The idea of helping such criminals and terrorists was distasteful to the US, to say the least. However, the possibility that these same criminals and terrorists might gain access to Syria's chemical weapons arsenal in the event of a rebel victory was far worse. That was the *real* reason Cross's Shadow Squadron had been mobilized to Syria.

Based out of the neighboring and allied country of Jordan, the eight-man team conducted special reconnaissance and direct-action raids against locations in rebel-controlled Syria. Their goal was to limit Al-Nusra's extremist influence on the Syrian revolution. To that end, Shadow Squadron had been coordinating with special operators from Israel to monitor the location of Syria's chemical weapons. While they didn't work side-by-side with Israeli soldiers, they regularly traded information on persons of interest or rumors concerning chemical-weaponry parts.

One of these trades of information led Cross's fireteam to Al-Haffah early this morning. An agent from Mossad — Israel's Intelligence Division — had arranged a trade of information that Cross was assigned to retrieve. Cross was used to being kept in the dark while deep inside unfriendly territory, but he wasn't especially thrilled about it.

Cross turned to Second Lieutenant Aram Jannati, another

Army Ranger. "I want you with Yamashita on overwatch," he said, handing over a tablet computer he'd been carrying.

"Sir," Jannati said, accepting the tactical pad from Cross.

With a tap on the screen, Jannati brought up a black-and-white image transmitted from the unmanned aerial vehicle (or UAV) hovering silently overhead. It had been following them ever since the fireteam set out. The UAV's low-light mini-camera provided a crisp, colorless image of the surrounding area. It showed no obvious sign of civilians or nearby hostiles.

Jannati turned the tablet screen toward Yamashita. "Where do you want to set up?" he asked.

"Here," Yamashita said after thinking for a moment. He tapped the image of a half-destroyed roof on a two-story house. It sat on a hill a block from their destination. Jannati nodded.

"Go," Cross said. He tapped the two-way canalphone nestled in his left ear. "High Road, this is Low Road. We need you to reposition Four-Eyes for us."

"Roger, this is Low Road," Staff Sergeant Edgar Brighton's voice replied in Cross's ear over the comm channel. Brighton was a technical genius and a Combat Controller from the US Air Force. He had designed the small quad-copter UAV, and now he piloted it remotely from where the rest of Shadow Squadron waited. "Just tell me where you want it."

Cross relayed new coordinates as Yamashita and Jannati relocated to their overwatch position. That left Cross alone with Hospital Corpsman Second Class Kyle Williams, the team's medic. "Are we expecting to need cover out there, sir?" Williams asked.

"You know what I know," Cross said. "There shouldn't be anybody out there except for our contacts and maybe a few scavengers. Still, better to have cover and not need it than to need it and not have it."

"Fair enough," Williams said. "But what's so important we need to go pick it up in person?"

Cross shook his head. "Command wouldn't say. Either the Israelis didn't tell them, or it's above our pay grade."

Williams tried to hide a frown, but Cross saw it. He felt the same way Williams did. In his experience, dealing with the Mossad was pretty much like dealing with the CIA. Both organizations tended to give out only as much information as it took to get soldiers like Cross and his men in trouble.

"We're in position," Jannati informed Cross.

"Four-Eyes is ready too," Brighton reported.

"Route's clear to the objective," Jannati added. "We'll let you know if that changes."

Cross acknowledged the reports with a quick double-tap on his canalphone. He nodded to Williams, and the two-man team set out.

They crept slowly through the shadows cast by the twisted bones of the ruined neighborhood. The men kept their M4 carbines at the ready, but they saw no signs of life except for a scrawny dog sniffing among some overturned trash cans.

From far and near came the rumble of exploding bombs and the crackle of distant gunfire. Sneaking through the eerie ghost town, Cross realized how glad he was that his own country hadn't descended into modern-day civil war. It was the stuff of nightmares.

The rendezvous point was a house at the end of a cul-de-sac. It had escaped direct shelling and gunfire but had still been seriously damaged. At some point, a bomb had exploded near a car parked in the street, hurling the smashed vehicle into the front of the house like a knife. The wrecked car jutted upside-down from the wall by the front door.

"The back is clear," Jannati informed them over the canalphone.

Cross double-tapped his acknowledgement and led Williams around the back. No lights were on inside and no sounds came from within. Cross paused at the threshold and motioned for Williams to take a position beside the rear door. Then Cross gave three quick knocks.

A moment later, a voice spoke from inside. "Jingle bells."

Cross gave a little smirk. "Batman smells," he answered, giving the agreed-upon password. Williams rolled his eyes.

"Wait," the inside voice said.

Cross heard rattling from a makeshift barricade being moved. Then the door opened. A young Israeli in black fatigues held a sawed-off shotgun pointed at gut level. He looked Cross and Williams over with obvious confusion, noticing the lack of any identifying marks on their uniforms. "You're the Americans. Are you CIA?"

"Nope," Cross said. "Do you have some intel for us?"

"Inside," the Israeli said, backing off and lowering his shotgun. He disappeared into the house, prompting Cross and Williams to follow him. Williams closed the door behind them.

"I'm glad you made it," the Israeli soldier said. "Which one of you is the medic?"

"I am," Williams answered.

"Our orders didn't mention anything about a medic," Cross said. It was sheer chance that he'd picked Williams to accompany him to the house.

The Israeli sighed. "So this isn't a rescue?" he asked. He paused at the threshold of an interior room. "I should've known."

"What's your name? Are you hurt?" Williams asked. "Do you need a medic?"

"My name is Benjamin," the man said, "and I'm fine. It's Asher who's injured. He's been shot." He turned and entered a nearby room.

Williams pushed past Cross and hurried into the next room with the Israeli. On a cot lay a second Israeli, who'd been stripped to the waist and heavily bandaged around his stomach with cut-up bedsheets. Williams knelt at the man's bedside and slung off his pack. The first Israeli leaned against the wall and looked down at his wounded comrade with a tired look of concern.

"Hey, Asher, can you hear me?" Williams asked. He lay one palm over the wounded man's forehead and took his pulse at the wrist with his other hand. The man lay immobile and unconscious. Sweat gleamed on his skin, and a dark bruise peeked above the topmost edge of the bandage. "He's burning up." He looked up at the first Israeli. "Where was he hit, Benjamin?"

"In his back," Benjamin said. "On the right."

"Commander, please give me a hand," Williams said.

Cross knelt beside Williams. Together they levered Asher onto his left side. At Williams' nod, Cross cut away the bandage until only a thick square of gauze remained over the wound site. Deep, purple-red bruises covered most of the wounded man's lower back.

"Hold that there," Williams said. "No exit wound. Severe bruising. Non-responsive. How long ago did this happen?"

Benjamin took a moment to realize Williams was speaking to him. "Oh, yesterday. What time is it?" He checked his watch. "Maybe 24 hours ago. A little longer."

Williams winced. "That's not good," he said. He dug through his medical pack and produced a set of fresh bandages.

"What happened?" Cross asked.

"Stupid, blind carelessness," Benjamin said. "We were in the mountains in Salma, monitoring a rebel cell. They were celebrating a victory and we were backing off to exfiltrate. We didn't realize they'd called up reinforcements to replace the losses they'd taken. We stumbled right into them, and they cut my team down. Asher and I got out and played *machboim* with them for a while until we found this place. They didn't seem too eager to follow us in here."

"Machboim?" Cross said.

"Hide and seek," Benjamin explained. "Anyway, when we got here I cleaned the wound and patched him up. I didn't think it was that bad at first. He just had a little bruising around the hole and very little bleeding. I thought we could wait for a rescue, but he's been getting worse all day."

"That's because he's bleeding internally," Williams said. He pressed his fingers hard into Asher's abdomen on the right side. The bruised flesh barely gave in at all. "See how rigid that is? His whole abdominal cavity is filling up with blood. He's got a high fever, which indicates a severe infection. His pulse is weak and he's barely breathing. He doesn't react when I poke him like this, which should hurt like crazy."

"Can you take the bullet out?" Benjamin asked, trying to stay calm. "Will that help?"

"Judging from where it went in," Williams said, "it's probably at least nicked his liver, his spleen, or his kidney. For all I know it's sitting inside one of those organs like a cork. It's a miracle he's lasted as long as he has."

"Is there anything you can do?" Benjamin asked. "At all?"

Williams put on a calm and professional expression. Cross had seen it once before in the field — the day Second Lieutenant Neil Larssen had been killed in action during a covert op on an oil platform in the Gulf of Mexico.

"I'm sorry," Williams said. "It would've been unlikely even if you could've gotten him straight to a hospital."

Benjamin's face darkened. "His sisters will be devastated."

Cross backed off to give the Israeli a moment to feel his grief. He quietly tapped his canalphone. "High Road, this is Low Road," Cross said. "We need a pickup for two friendlies, one injured."

"Injured?" Brighton's voice replied in Cross's ear. "Who?"

"Not one of ours," Cross said. "We're taking them back to our base."

Cross double-tapped his canalphone to clear the channel. "Overwatch," he said, "reel in and get ready for pickup."

"Sir," Yamashita and Jannati replied.

Benjamin stood. "Where will you take us?" he asked Cross.

"Home," Cross said, "with a brief stop at our base. We'll do everything we can for your man, I promise you that. But you'll owe us some information for the extraction."

"I'll tell you whatever you want to know," Benjamin said. He watched Williams finish bandaging his comrade's wounds.

When Williams was finished, Benjamin crouched in the medic's place. He placed his hand on Asher's chest and hung his head. Quietly and calmly, he murmured an Arabic prayer for the dead and dying over his comrade's body.

Cross walked over to Williams and stood beside him. "He's not going to make it?" Cross asked, barely above a whisper.

The medic shook his head. "He's lost too much blood, Commander," Williams said. "They're not going to be able to do anything for him back at base that I can't just do here."

"Such as?" Cross asked.

Williams let out a small sigh. "Load him up with morphine to ease his suffering," he said.

Cross grunted. "All right. Our ride back to base is going to be here in a few minutes. Get Asher ready to move, and ease his suffering as much as you can." He lowered his voice. "But save the morphine. We're not home safe yet, and one of our men might still need it."

"Yessir," Williams said. "I just hope whatever intel these guys found was worth it."

"Me too," Cross said.

* * *

Several hours later, Shadow Squadron had returned to its temporary base in Jordan.

Asher, the wounded Mossad agent, had died in transport. The Americans put his body on a plane back home to Israel. The other agent, Benjamin, agreed to an intensive interview with Cross and Cross's superiors via two-way satellite broadcast. The intel Benjamin's team had gathered filled the gaps in information collected by Cross's team. All the data went to a crack team of analysts back at Command. That analysis painted a terrifying picture.

Cross called in the rest of Shadow Squadron for a briefing. The team convened in the mess hall stuck onto the meager barracks they'd borrowed from the Jordanian army. Cross set up a palm-size projector on the end of the mess table. He synced it to the tactical tablet computer cradled under his arm.

Cross quickly glanced across the room to make sure everyone was present. He tapped his tablet's screen. The projector displayed an image on the wall beside him. Chief Walker shut the door and took a position on the opposite side of the projection.

Normally Cross preferred Walker to sit with the men during a mission briefing, but this time he didn't mind the extra support up front.

"Well this can't be good news," Brighton whispered to Yamashita. "Walker and Cross aren't even glaring at each other."

Yamashita ignored him.

"We have a serious problem," Cross said. "An emergency interrupt just came down from Command. We're going mobile in one hour for a White Needle emergency."

Eyes widened on every face in the room. White Needle was code for a rogue chemical weapon and implied that it was in the hands of an enemy with intent to use it.

"Give them the background, Chief," Cross said, handing the tablet over to Walker. "The short version."

"Sir," Walker said, taking the tablet. He swiped away the first image to replace it with a dossier photo of an olive-skinned, bearded man in his late 50s. "You all remember our target, Abdul-mateen Shenwari. He's an Afghani militant who was behind bombings and raids in Afghanistan, Yemen, and Iraq. Intel confirms that he's up to more of the same stuff in Syria. He's organizing cells of FSA fighters against President Assad's army."

Nods and low murmurs went around the room. Shadow Squadron had originally been tracking Shenwari in Iraq, but a rash of bad intel had allowed the criminal terrorist to slip through their fingers. When CIA informants declared that Shenwari had resurfaced in Syria, Cross's team had been reassigned there to help with ongoing operations. But Shenwari always remained one step ahead and just out of reach.

"Intel from our Israeli friend helped us identify the top two locals working under Shenwari here in Syria," Walker said. He advanced the image on the tactical pad, breaking out two more dossier photos beneath Shenwari's photo. Both photos were taken secretly, as neither man seemed aware of the fact that he was being photographed. Both photos showed lean, hard-faced Syrian men.

"The first one is Baltasar Dyab," Cross explained. "He's commanding a raid on an artillery emplacement overlooking the mountain town of Salma in the Latakia Governorate."

Walker nodded, then tapped the tactical pad. A map of the northwestern coast of Syria appeared. The towns of Salma and Latakia were highlighted on the map.

"The Syrian Army's been raining shells and missiles on the city of Salma for months," Walker said. "So the rebels taking control of the emplacement is a pretty important local victory."

Walker advanced the image on the screen once more. A picture of Shenwari's other local lieutenant appeared. "Our Israeli friend was also able to confirm something we'd suspected but hadn't been able to prove," Walker said. "Last week, FSA rebels ambushed a supply convoy en route from Latakia. We knew that Shenwari's other top local man was behind the raid, but we didn't know much more than that. Now we do. The convoy was en route from a chemical munitions facility in the city, moving sarin gas to a secondary location. We thought the convoy and all its materiel had been destroyed, but Mossad's information indicates that the FSA actually made off with a large amount of sarin gas. Enough for a single warhead."

"How long have they known about this?" Yamashita asked with a scowl. "Surely not since before the raid."

"We believe they did," Cross said grimly.

"They knew this last week? And they're only just telling us now?" Brighton asked. "What the heck were they waiting for?"

"They might not have told us anything at all if we hadn't extracted their men from Al-Haffah," Jannati said.

"So they knew their men needed extraction," Yamashita said. "They just called it an 'information drop.'"

"Didn't they think we'd help if they just asked?" Brighton asked. "I don't know if that's devious or lazy or —"

"But where's the connection?" Staff Sergeant Paxton asked, cutting in. "Between the convoy ambush and Salma, I mean."

Cross took the tactical pad from Walker. He gave Paxton a grateful nod for getting things back on track. "All available evidence suggests that Shenwari has ordered his two lieutenants to regroup their forces in Salma with the sarin gas," Cross said. "Hence our White Needle emergency. Our own intel indicates they are planning to arm and launch a chemical warhead from the artillery position the FSA just captured. And signs point to sooner rather than later, before Assad's army can take back control of that emplacement."

"What's the range of their warhead from that position?" Paxton asked.

Cross swiped across his tactical pad and brought up a map of western Syria. The towns of Salma and Latakia were surrounded by a progression of rings that expanded out into the neighboring cities, as well as into Turkey to the north. Centers of high population density within those rings were all marked on the map, as well as important Syrian Army military bases and Turkish refugee camps to the North.

"As you can see," Cross said, "their range of attack is alarmingly large."

"How do we know they're planning to use what they have?" Sergeant Shepherd asked. "I don't see how it would benefit them. The western world is already on their side. Everybody's worried President Assad is going to use these things on his own civilians. What could the rebels gain from using the warhead?"

"It's Shenwari we're worried about," Cross said. "He's radical and unstable and dedicated to his jihadi cause. If he's got a weapon like this, he will use it — it's just a matter of time. Fortunately, our intelligence is ahead of the curve, so we've got a chance to stop him."

Cross leaned forward. "So we're heading to Salma to neutralize Shenwari's chemical weapon capacity," he said. "If we can recover the weapon or weapons, great. If not, we're authorized to destroy them. As a secondary objective, we're to kill or capture Shenwari if he's at the site. If not, we're to scoop up one or both of his lieutenants for questioning."

"Sounds simple enough," Yamashita said. "Are we coordinating with the Israelis on this?"

Cross and Walker both shook their heads. Cross kept his expression blank, but Walker's face betrayed some of the frustration both men felt.

"The Israelis are staying out of this one," Cross said tightly. "They say they've already lost too many men putting the puzzle pieces together for us."

Cross swiped and tapped on his tablet screen to bring up low-light camera footage taken from a high vantage point. It showed recent images of the Syrian Army's artillery emplacement in the mountains near Salma. They gave the team a decent idea of the emplacement's layout and size.

"That's footage from the Avenger UAV," Brighton said.

"Correct," Cross said, clearly impressed that Brighton could identify the UAV solely by its photos. "It was taken a week ago — before the raid. We're trying to get a UAV or a satellite over the area to provide fresher intel, but this is the best we can do at the moment."

Cross produced a laser pointer from his hip pocket. He shined it on the southern portion of the map. "We'll be inserting via Wraith from this direction..."

* * *

Within the hour, the team was in the air, aboard its Wraith stealth helicopter. A heavily modified Sikorsky Blackhawk, the Wraith used state-of-the-art scythe-shaped rotors, a radar-deflecting surface, and a host of other top-secret innovations. The Wraith was almost impossible to see in the night sky, detect on radar, or even hear unless it was right overhead. The muffled engine noise and reduced propeller turbulence made for an eerie stillness inside the passenger compartment, except for a strange humming sound. Cross had ridden in the Wraith before, but the unnerving hum still got under his skin.

"Go over the safety briefing again, Williams," Cross said. "Humor me."

"Sir," Williams half-said, half-sighed. He leaned forward on his bench seat. "The chemical in our White Needle is sarin. It's clear, odorless, and tasteless. You can be exposed to it through your skin, your eyes, or through respiration. It's heavier than air, so if it gets loose, it's going to roll right downhill."

"Right toward us," Brighton said. His insect-like night-vision mask sat atop his head, leaving his expression clearly visible. Although he had a smile on his face, it looked sickly and strained.

"Yes," Williams said. "And it acts fast that so you're going to have to watch yourselves and each other for symptoms."

"And if you do notice symptoms," Cross added, "tell me immediately so we can get out of the area."

"Right," Williams said. "The signs to watch out for are: runny nose, watery eyes, drooling, sweating, headache, blurred vision, eye pain, cough, chest tightness, confusion, weakness, nausea..."

Cross nodded and let Williams trail off. What Williams didn't point out was that those symptoms indicated a relatively mild exposure to sarin. Higher concentrations of the deadly chemical would result in convulsions, paralysis, loss of consciousness, and respiratory failure — all within just a few seconds. At that point, there would be nothing Williams could do for them, so it was best not to fill their heads with fear.

"Just out of curiosity, Commander," Brighton asked, "why aren't we doing this mission in full-on rubber chemical suits?"

None of Cross's men had voiced this question before now. Apparently they trusted that their commanding officer had a compelling reason.

"For one thing," Cross said, "the odds of us coming in contact with actual sarin gas are minimal. The components Shenwari's locals stole are binary. They remain separate and harmless until the warhead mechanism mixes them into sarin in flight. If they do launch it via missile, we're not the ones who are going to have to worry about the gas."

Brighton and the others nodded. Apparently the explanation set their minds at ease, even if it shouldn't have.

"Second," Cross continued, "this artillery emplacement is up in the coastal mountains, and we're going to be inserting downslope via Wraith to preserve the element of surprise. That means we're going to goat-foot it upslope, and take it from me — you do not want to do that in a full chemical suit. The lighter we travel, the faster we move, the sooner we get the job done."

"All right, Commander," Brighton said. "That makes sense." He paused for a moment then turned to Williams. "But you're stocked up on whatever the antidote for sarin is, right?"

"I'm stocked up on atropine sulfate and diazepam," Williams said, patting his first-aid kit. Cross knew that wasn't exactly the cure that Williams made it out to be.

"He can also provide you with a lollipop if you don't cry too much," Shepherd said, grinning, as he dug an elbow into Brighton's ribs.

Williams chuckled. "They're sugar-free," he added.

"Blech," Brighton said, sticking out his tongue. "I'd rather have the sarin."

"Quiet down," Cross said over the laughter. "We're just a couple minutes out from the LZ. Get squared away. It's almost time."

"Sir," the men murmured. Their faces turned hard and serious. Cross was glad for the break in the tension — he could always count on Staff Sergeant Brighton to provide one. But this was no longer the time for jokes.

* * *

The Wraith reached its destination and hovered high above the artillery emplacement occupied by FSA rebels.

"Bird's eye is coming online now, Commander Cross," the helicopter pilot said through Cross's canalphone.

"Roger that," Cross said. "We're syncing up with you now."

Brighton tapped then swiped the tablet computer in his lap. A live feed from the helicopter's powerful fiber-optic cameras came on line. It wasn't as good as the feed would have been from Brighton's own Four-Eyes, but high winds over the mountains had forced them to leave his UAV behind. As the image became clear, Brighton looked up at Cross and gave him a thumb's up.

"We have a visual," Cross said. "Stand by to take us to the landing zone."

"Roger that," the helicopter pilot said. "Now approaching the LZ."

"Huddle up," Cross said, half-joking. The interior compartment of the Wraith was hardly spacious when packed full of eight soldiers and their gear.

Cross motioned for Brighton to hand him the tablet. He positioned it so all the men could see it. Cross switched the overhead camera footage into a wide-angle view of the terrain. He overlaid it with contour lines showing the area's relative elevation. The overtaken Syrian artillery emplacement was little more than a flat, rocky ridge at the top of a gently sloping path. A flimsy wooden cabin had been erected there at some point, likely to provide sleeping quarters for the artillery crew, but tents had since surrounded it. Three M116 75mm pack howitzers stood at the ready by the edge of the ridge. A flatbed truck that had likely transported the weapons was visible next to the tents. FSA rebels lingered around the howitzers, but they didn't appear to be tending the weapons or preparing to operate them. There was no sign of ammunition for the weapons.

Between the howitzers and the nearby mortars was another truck, which drew most of Cross's attention. The boxy, eight-wheeled brick of a vehicle had a long, steel rail structure on top. A crane apparatus reached down over one side. Beside the truck, being lifted by the crane, was a 30-foot-long steel missile. The missile was a 9K52 Luna-M, more commonly referred to as a FROG-7. It had an effective range of 70 to 90 kilometers and could travel at a top speed of three times the speed of sound. In other words, the target would never hear it coming.

Most importantly, the FROG-7 was capable of launching a chemical warhead. And from what Cross could tell, the men clustering around the FROG-7 were preparing to deliver just such a warhead to some unsuspecting target. When the men in the Wraith realized this, they started to fidget anxiously.

"Okay, then," Cross said. He tapped his canalphone to include the Wraith's pilot in what he had to say. "Guys, plan one is out. They're getting ready to launch down there, so we're escalating this to a full-court press. Our main objective is to disable that missile — and anybody who tries to get anywhere near it."

"I'm packing two Hellfire missiles, Commander," the Wraith pilot informed him. "I can blast that launcher apart from up here, if you like."

"The Hellfires don't burn hot enough," Cross said. "I can't risk a detonation throwing liquid sarin all down the mountainside and into the city of Salma."

"I suppose that's a fair point, Commander," the pilot said, his voice full of disappointment. "Negative on the Hellfires."

Cross smirked. "Actually, go ahead and put one into those howitzers," he said. "They should be far enough from the FROG-7 to minimize the danger."

"I can do that," the pilot chirped.

"After that I want a quick sweep with the miniguns across the open ground. Then get us down and let us out. Fast. You can hop back up here when we're clear."

"You got it," the pilot said.

"Guy sure seems to like his artillery," Brighton joked.

"I heard that," the pilot said.

"Chief Walker," Cross said, "I want you, Shepherd, Brighton, and Jannati out of the Wraith and down first. Yamashita and I will cover you while you sweep a space clear for us to follow. When we're down, we'll make for the FROG-7 and eliminate the surrounding resistance. Once it's ours, Brighton will disarm and disengage the FROG-7's warhead. Then we hold position until the Wraith comes back and gets us outta there."

"Sounds simple enough," Chief Walker said sarcastically.

Cross didn't blame him. He knew that as soon as he gave the order, his simple, straightforward backup plan would become an exercise in barely constrained chaos. Fortunately, Shadow Squadron had the element of surprise on their side.

"All right," Cross said. "Everyone knows what they need to do?"

The men nodded. "Roger that," the Wraith's pilot added through the canalphone.

Cross's heart rate sped up. The sour and cold taste of surging adrenaline made his lips peel back in a wild, involuntary grin.

"Let's do it," Cross said.

The Wraith descended in a wide, spiraling arc with its nose pointed toward the rocky ridge. Recessed panels on the Wraith's underside folded open, revealing two Hellfire missiles. At the pilot's click of a switch, one of the missiles lanced down into the cluster of unmanned pack howitzers.

The howitzers exploded in a blaze of heat and thunder. Their twisted wreckage flew off the ridge and down the mountainside.

The pilot spun the Wraith in midair and launched the second (and last) Hellfire missile into the cluster of mortars on the other side of the emplacement. The smaller, lighter mortars disappeared in a cloud of billowing smoke and earth. No wreckage was left behind. The vehicles parked near the mortars were damaged beyond repair, as well.

The pilot's assault couldn't have caused more confusion and panic. Rebels dashed out of their tents and cabin and began running in all directions with their weapons drawn, trying and failing to find the source of the attack. To clarify the situation for them, the pilot made his presence more than obvious by opening fire with a pair of M-134 miniguns.

The miniguns laid down two tight streams of 7.62x51mm NATO rounds at a rate of nearly 50 rounds per second. The sun-bright lines of tracer rounds and the vicious power of the regular rounds scattered the soldiers. Not all of them were able to get to safety.

All the while, the Wraith descended toward the side of the emplacement that was farthest from the mountain road. When the chopper reached a safe height, it opened its doors and dropped a pair of rappelling ropes from each side. Walker, Shepherd, Brighton, and Jannati were already clipped onto the ropes to descend. Cross and Yamashita stepped forward and knelt in the opening next to the others.

"Go!" Cross ordered.

The first four-man fireteam stepped out of the Wraith and slid quickly down their ropes. Cross and Yamashita provided covering fire with their M4 carbines, picking off those few fighters below who had stood their ground and fired up at the helicopter. The two best shots in Shadow Squadron, Cross and Yamashita easily kept their fellow soldiers safe all the way to the ground.

The four men below unclipped themselves from the lines and formed up to move toward the FROG-7 launcher.

"Ready up!" Cross ordered. Then he, Williams, Yamashita, and Paxton clipped onto the ropes and dropped out of the Wraith to join their comrades.

As Cross's group slid down, those already on the ground took a knee and laid down suppressing fire. Walker and Jannati fired in three-round bursts from their M4 carbines. Brighton let loose with more intimidating and less precise blasts from his AA-12 combat shotgun, chewing up the side of the cabin where some of the gunmen had taken cover.

The most effective cover fire came from Shepherd. He

tucked his M240 machine gun under one arm like a madman and swept it in an arc across the area. It was a terrible firing position for a belt-fed machine gun, but it was undeniably effective at backing off the enemy force.

"To the FROG-7!" Cross said as his second team touched down and unclipped from the rappelling lines. A high-speed winch slurped the lines back up into the Wraith, and the helicopter disappeared into the night sky.

Brighton pointed toward the wreckage where the mortars and the rebels' parking lot had been. "RPG!" he shouted. The team turned to see a man with a rocket-propelled grenade launcher aimed at the Wraith.

Cross and Yamashita both fired with their M4s. Their target jerked and fell, pulling the trigger just as his legs went out from under him. A line of white smoke shot upward through the air, missing the Wraith by mere yards.

"Yikes!" the pilot yelped in Cross's canalphone. "Thanks, fellas!"

"All clear, Wraith," Cross and Yamashita replied. They glanced at each other and cracked a quick grin.

"Go!" Cross ordered.

As one, Shadow Squadron rushed across the emplacement, dodging fire from the few FSA fighters who'd taken cover.

Shepherd kept the shooters pinned down with machine gun fire as he and Paxton brought up the rear. Unfortunately, a group of FSA soldiers had taken cover by the FROG-7, which Cross didn't realize until his men were right up on it.

Two men popped out from behind the heavy truck to open fire with AK-47s. Brighton managed to nail one of them with a thunderous blast from his AA-12, throwing the man back against one of the launcher's tires. The other squeezed his rifle's trigger, spraying automatic fire.

The rounds hit Walker, Jannati, and Williams before a three-round burst from Cross cut the second gunman down. Walker was hit in the lower leg. Jannati caught two bullets in his ballistic vest. The last shot punched through Williams' upper right arm, missing his chest by less than an inch. Walker and Williams both cursed roughly. Jannati would have done the same if the shots hadn't knocked the wind out of him.

Cross ordered his team to establish a defensive perimeter and to secure the FROG-7 and its loader. Shepherd and Paxton took a position behind a line of waist-high rocks. They set up the M240 machine gun and opened up with it. Yamashita knelt beside them and added his deadly single-shot cover fire to Shepherd's more manic automatic fire. As the FSA fighters' return fire turned erratic, Paxton popped up and hurled an M67 frag grenade into the wooden cabin.

The explosion rattled the structure and blew out its last remaining window. He threw a second grenade into the nest of ruined vehicles where most of the FSA rebels had taken refuge. In the wake of the second detonation, enemy fire ceased. Murmuring voices and the whimpers of the wounded could be heard in the darkness, but no one seemed too eager to engage Shadow Squadron anymore.

While Shepherd, Paxton, and Yamashita were doing their work, the other five members of the team had their hands full securing the FROG-7. The rebels had finished loading the missile onto its launcher before Shadow Squadron had touched ground, and a team of tenacious gunmen had holed up around the machine to defend it. Two of those fighters had surprised the squad and wounded Williams and Walker. At least two more men remained alive on the opposite side of the launcher.

As Williams helped Walker hobble over to the launcher, Brighton rushed over to them and helped Williams break out his first-aid kit. Jannati, meanwhile, shook his head clear and gulped down a deep, ragged breath. He'd found himself taking a knee next to the body of the man Brighton had shot. The body belonged to Sargon Balhous — one of Shenwari's top local lieutenants.

When Jannati had his breathing under control, Cross motioned for him to get up and move with him. Cross then motioned for Brighton to stay with Williams to aid and cover the medic while he tended to the injuries. Brighton gave a quick nod and hefted his AA-12 at the ready.

Cross led Jannati to the corner of the launcher and paused at the edge to listen. He heard two voices conversing in Arabic in desperate, rushed whispers. Cross heard the click-clacking of a computer keyboard and was able to make out the word "coordinates" and the Arabic phrase "*Allahu yaghefiru liy.*"

Cross signaled for Jannati to follow him, then he vaulted over the high bumper of the FROG-7 truck and sprang around the corner at a high angle. Jannati came around a second later at ground level. The two FSA fighters on that side of the truck were ready for some sort of attack, but Cross's unconventional tactic caught them off-guard. The quicker of the two FSA men fired where Cross's chest should have been. Instead the shot hit only the empty air between his knees.

Cross shot the soldier in the shoulder and Jannati emerged a second later to finish him off. The second man was crouched over a mobile data terminal that was plugged into the side of the FROG-7 truck. Cross's second shot missed him by inches.

The man — none other than Shenwari's other local lieutenant, Baltasar Dyab — mashed one last key on the data terminal. He looked up at Cross and Jannati with an expression of hopelessness. Tears gleamed in his eyes as he spread his hands and backed away from the keyboard.

Jannati raised his rifle and growled, "What did you —"

A moment later, the roar of the FROG-7's rocket answered Jannati's question. Heat, pressure, and an unbelievable roar obliterated the capacity for rational thought. Cross and Jannati could only watch helplessly as a 30-foot-long missile loaded with sarin gas roared upward into the night.

"*Allahu yaghefiru liy*," Dyab murmured. He was staring at the ground as the missile accelerated into the sky. He repeated the phrase over and over again.

Jannati raised his weapon to shoot the man down, but Cross raised a hand to stop him.

"Balhous is dead," Cross said. "We need this one alive if we're going to find Shenwari."

Jannati scowled. "Fine. I'll wrap him up." He ordered Dyab to lie down on his stomach and put his hands behind his back. The FSA fighter did so without complaining. He just kept muttering the same phrase over and over as Jannati bound his wrists with a zip-cuff from his pocket.

"Brighton, get over here!" Cross yelled.

Brighton had already come around the truck. He snapped his wraparound night-vision system up over his head. His eyes were saucer-wide.

"The rocket's up," Cross said, his voice flat but strained. "Can you ——"

"Where's it headed?" Brighton asked. "I mean, Israel and Damascus are that way. Turkey's in the south" He pointed north. "And nothing's west of here except the ocean."

"It's going into Saraqeb," Baltasar Dyab interrupted. "*Allahu yaghefiru liy.*"

"Saraqeb's rebel-held, you idiot!" Jannati snapped, tightening the zip-cuffs on his prisoner's wrists.

"Can you stop it?" Cross asked Brighton. "Blow it up, turn it around, or something?"

"Not from here, man," Brighton said. "The FROG-7's not a guided missile. This launcher's not a remote control. It's just a big truck with a rail on top. That's all."

"What can stop it?" Cross said. "The Wraith?"

"The Wraith won't be able to intercept it," Brighton said. "Do we have any Patriot missiles nearby?"

Cross shook his head.

"Then I don't know," Brighton said, looking sick. "How about a miracle? Anybody owe you one of those?"

Cross grabbed Brighton by the shoulders and held him face to face. "People are going to die, Sergeant. They're counting on you. I'm counting on you. There must be *something* you can do to stop that thing!"

Brighton looked terrified. Cross forced himself to take a deep breath. He was only making things worse, and they were rapidly running out of time. If that warhead was heading for Saraqeb, they only had a few minutes to do something about it.

"Ed," Cross said slowly and calmly. "You can do this. If anybody can solve this problem, you can. So work it out. What do you need to get that missile out of the air? Nothing's off the table. Just name it and I'll make it happen."

Brighton closed his eyes and took a deep breath. He thought hard for what seemed an eternity of precious seconds. Then his eyes flew open. "Where's the Avenger?"

Cross felt a glimmer of hope. The Avenger was a modified General Atomics MQ-1 Predator Drone. It had high-quality cameras, a powerful engine, radar-deflecting stealth fuselage, and an array of missiles. Only the CIA and the Joint Special Operations Command knew it even existed.

"It's over Aleppo," Cross said, his excitement growing alongside Brighton's. "Is that close enough?" Aleppo, the largest city in Syria, was only 25 miles from Saraqeb.

"It'll be tight," Brighton said. "Get it moving toward us, then get me control of it. I'll bring that missile down."

"Command," Cross barked, opening the emergency channel over his canalphone. "I need a hotlink feed from the Avenger's camera to my team's tactical pad and a secure line to Colonel Max Gordon in Colorado."

As Cross began sorting things out through channels, Brighton took the tactical pad out and plugged it into the truck's mobile data terminal. When he had them linked up, his fingers flew over the keyboard. Soon he had established a connection via satellite link to the US Air Force base back in Colorado where the top-secret Avenger unmanned aircraft was remotely piloted. He accepted the Command-approved feed from the Avenger's cameras, but he hit a brick wall when he tried to access the drone's flight controls.

"I can't get in!" he cried. Hacking a top-secret Air Force command center with the equipment he had on hand just wasn't realistic.

"Gordon, listen to me!" Cross said to the man on the other end of the comm channel. "I don't have time for this. This is a White Needle emergency and a Shadow-tier mission. Your people don't have security clearance for this. Just get us access to that UAV. *Now!*"

A moment later, Cross nodded. He looked at Brighton. "Okay, he needs to know our —"

"Just make him tell Lieutenant Wallace in their Security Department to stop fighting me," Brighton interrupted. "I can do the rest from here."

Cross relayed the information. He moved to stand behind Brighton. The moment Colonel Gordon complied and allowed Brighton access to the Avenger's flight controls, Brighton stood up straight. He held the tactical pad out in front of him in both hands like a car steering wheel. The screen showed a front-facing camera view along with a complicated HUD that Cross could barely decipher.

"Got it!" Brighton said. "Interface is up, tablet's synced. Holy crap, I'm flying the Avenger!"

Cross marveled at what Brighton had been able to accomplish in less than a minute. By tilting and turning the tactical tablet, he was able to control the pitch, yaw, and roll of the Avenger UAV. Through an interface on the touchscreen, he also had control of acceleration and the weapons system. The interface was crude, but it was good enough for the problem at hand. Brighton oriented the tablet, aiming the armed drone in the right direction. Then he opened the accelerator all the way up. Cross watched in amazement as the Avenger streaked westward from the Aleppo Governorate tearing across the sky toward Saraqeb.

"This won't take more than a minute, Commander," Brighton said.

"That's all the time we've got," Cross said. He stepped away from Brighton to check on the rest of his men. Jannati had led Dyab around to the other side of the launcher truck. Williams was directing Walker how to properly bandage the bullet wound in Williams' arm. A heavy bandage was already wrapped around Walker's calf.

"Report," Cross said.

"Area secure, sir," Walker said. It was ostensibly good news, but Walker's expression was clouded by a faint scowl. All along, Walker had made no secret of the fact that he wasn't happy having to potentially shoot and kill FSA rebels, even in the name of a greater good. "The rebels have all bugged out. The ones left alive, anyway."

"Good." Cross gave a whistle at the small covering fireteam of Yamashita, Shepherd, and Paxton. "Hey, guys, reel in. Get hands under these two and get ready for evacuation." He turned back to Walker. "Call the Wraith back in."

"Sir," Walker said.

Cross came back around the truck to find Brighton staring hard at the tactical tablet. His fingers were white-knuckled from gripping too hard.

"Breathe, Sergeant," Cross said while peeking over Brighton's shoulder. At some point, Brighton had switched the display to a thermal readout. The pinpoints of stars were gone from the night sky, and the city heat of Saraqeb glowed like plankton on the sea's surface. And in the center of the screen was a white-hot point of heat: the FROG-7 rocket.

"Is that it?" Cross asked. "Take it down."

"It's not close enough yet, Commander," Brighton said through clenched teeth. "Give me a second. Just give me a second..."

Cross watched the screen from over Brighton's shoulder, feeling every bit as tense as Brighton was. The rocket began to tilt downward, so Brighton tilted the tablet slightly to cause the Avenger UAV to match it. Long, painful seconds went by, allowing the rocket to grow larger on the display. The lights of Saraqeb began to take up more and more of the screen.

"Brighton..." Cross urged.

"There!" Brighton shouted.

Brighton pressed his thumb down on the weapons overlay on the UAV's heads-up display, launching the Avenger's full complement of air-to-air Stinger missiles. Glowing streaks of fire filled the screen. They rapidly closed in on the FROG-7 rocket. Brighton and Cross held their breaths as the missiles closed in on their target...

...and missed.

"What?" Brighton yelped. "No way!"

"Tell me you've got more of those," Cross said, fighting to keep the sudden fear out of his voice. "Sergeant?"

"Everything else is air-to-ground," Brighton said with a shrug. "I'd never hit that tiny little thing." He frowned. "But there is one thing left I can try."

"Whatever it is, do it," Cross said.

"I'm already on it, Commander," Brighton said. "Just one quick question…how much did the Avenger cost?"

Cross was about to unleash his rage at what seemed to be another of Brighton's smart-aleck remarks. Then Cross realized what Brighton was getting at as he watched him maneuver the Avenger down below the oncoming rocket.

Cross moaned. "Twelve to fifteen million dollars," he said. "Do it."

"My condolences to their budgeting department," Brighton said. He pitched sharply back and upward. When the FROG-7 reappeared on the Avenger's camera display, it took up almost the entire screen. Then the feed from the Avenger disappeared.

Brighton had crashed the UAV into the rocket, destroying both devices harmlessly above Saraqeb.

He lowered the tactical tablet and looked up at Cross. His shocked, adrenaline-flared expression was an exact match for the way Cross felt.

When Brighton finally spoke, it was in a small, hushed voice. "I ain't paying for that, by the way."

"Me neither," Cross said just as quietly.

* * *

The Wraith carried Shadow Squadron and its prisoner back to the temporary base in Jordan. Dyab remained silent.

Even when Cross told him that Brighton had destroyed the rocket and its entire chemical payload with no loss of life, the FSA lieutenant didn't even look up from his lap.

Cross glared down at Baltasar Dyab. "Why did you launch the rocket at Saraqeb?"

Now the man did raise his eyes, but they were empty.

"Answer him!" Jannati barked, shoving Dyab from behind. He clutched his chest where the bullet had hit his vest.

"Why Saraqeb?" Cross asked again, with a quick scowl at Jannati to calm the man down. "It's still under FSA control. Why target them?"

"Shenwari," the prisoner answered. "He convinced us it was a worthy sacrifice."

"Worthy?" Jannati snapped. "Thirty-thousand people live in Saraqeb! Rebels and innocent civilians!"

"Martyrs," Dyab said, his tone hollow. "He said they would be rewarded in Heaven and that Syria would be free."

Jannati was speechless. Cross thought he understood what the Syrian meant, but he looked to Walker for an explanation.

"You weren't going to claim responsibility, right?" Walker Dyab. "You were going to leave that position as soon as the rocket was away. Then the entire world would think it was Assad's men who had fired it on your people."

"Yes," Dyab said. "Then the rest of you, watching but never involving yourselves, would have to help us. That's what

Shenwari said. Only he said you would reveal your true colors to the world by failing to help us. You would just make more excuses and —"

"Don't try to make this about us," Cross said. "It's not about us. It's not even about Shenwari, though he deserves some of the blame here. The fact of the matter is this: the horror we stopped here tonight is all on you. *You*, Dyab. You were the one who launched the rocket. You were the one who could've said no, but you didn't."

Dyab broke eye contact and hung his head. Whether he believed Cross or not, he gave no sign.

"*Allahu yaghefiru liy*," Dyab murmured, retreating back inside himself once again. "May God forgive me."

"We'll see," Cross told him. "We'll see."

MISSION DEBRIEFING

OPERATION

WHITE NEEDLE   5678

MISSION COMPLETE

PRIMARY OBJECTIVE

- Rendezvous with Israeli forces
- Recover missing chemical weapon

SECONDARY OBJECTIVES

- Capture Syrian rebels responsible
- x Limit enemy casualties

3245.98 ● ● ●

STATUS

3/4 COMPLETE

CROSS, RYAN

RANK: Lieutenant Commander
BRANCH: Navy SEAL
PSYCH PROFILE: Team leader
of Shadow Squadron. Control
oriented and loyal, Cross insisted
on hand-picking each member of
his squad.

Talk about a close call -- and an expensive one. I'm just thankful that Brighton was able to save the day. These things really need to stop coming down to the wire because my heart can't handle it.

I'm going to have to make this debriefing, well, brief since Command is on my case regarding operational expenses for this mission. Apparently "it was our only option" isn't a sufficient excuse for destroying a multi-million-dollar UAV. But I'll be sleeping well at night knowing how many lives we saved.

- Lieutenant Commander Ryan Cross

ERROR

UNAUTHORIZED

USER MUST HAVE LEVEL 12 CLEARANCE
OR HIGHER IN ORDER TO GAIN ACCESS
TO FURTHER MISSION INFORMATION.

2019.681

MISSION BRIEFING

OPERATION

PHANTOM SUN 5678

An unknown aircraft has crashed in Antarctica near a remote science facility. Shadow Squadron has been tasked with recovering the device. Early reports show that Russian Special Forces are already on the scene, meaning we need to keep a low profile and avoid hostilities if at all possible.

Upon landing, we'll rendezvous with a psy-ops spook from Phantom Cell who has more information on the situation. I don't need to remind you, gentlemen, that stealth is of paramount importance for this mission.

– Lieutenant Commander Ryan Cross

3245.96

ANTARCTICA

SOUTH POLE

PRIMARY OBJECTIVE

- Locate & secure crashed aircraft
- Maintain anonymity

SECONDARY OBJECTIVES

- Avoid hostilities with Russian
  Special Forces

1932.789

0412.981

1624.054

PHANTOM SUN

Lieutenant Commander Ryan Cross was proud and honored to serve as Shadow Squadron's commanding officer. But as the seven men under his direct command shuffled into the briefing room, they didn't give the impression that they shared his honor and pride in their work. In fact, they didn't look much like the squad of highly trained professionals that he knew they were. Right now, more than anything, they looked tired. It was just after 0500 hours local time, and none of them shared his enthusiasm for the dawn's early light.

The men filed in quietly with heavy eyes and slow footsteps, many of them clutching mugs of steaming coffee. Each of them carried English muffin sandwiches stuffed full of scrambled eggs, bacon, ham, cheese, and whatever else they could shovel in.

"All right, you herd of turtles," Walker grumbled as he came into the room. "Shuffle in and sit down."

Like Cross, Walker had come to Shadow Squadron from

the Navy SEALs, though his training had been more focused and specialized than Cross's. Walker had been with the team since the creation of the program. In the beginning, Walker had resented Cross's authority. Recently, however, Walker had grown to like Cross — and showed him respect on and off the battlefield.

Walker demonstrated that respect by coming into the briefing room balancing an extra breakfast sandwich on top of his own. He precariously clung to the handle of a second mug of coffee in his other hand. The Chief set the extra sandwich and coffee down in front of Cross, then took his position at the other corner.

"Thanks, Chief," Cross said. "You didn't have to do that." Cross neglected to add that he'd already eaten breakfast an hour ago.

"No problem," Walker grumbled, hunching over his coffee and avoiding eye contact with everyone. "So is there a reason we're having this briefing before we've even done PT?"

"Yep," Cross replied. He took a sip of coffee for the sake of politeness — it was pitch black, the way Walker liked it.

Cross tapped the touchscreen on the surface of the table. A section of the wall slid open to reveal a high-definition LED screen. It showed the swords-and-globe emblem of the Joint Special Operations Command. Another tap and swipe brought up a still image of two men wearing heavy, red snow parkas as they rode away on a snowmobile. The camera peered over the shoulder of another parka-clad individual on a second snowmobile. Both vehicles made their way across a desolate, white expanse of snow and ice under a gray sky.

At the sight of the image, Staff Sergeant Edgar Brighton gasped in excitement and immediately sucked a mouthful of his breakfast down the wrong pipe. He pointed at the screen, his eyes watering, as he coughed and choked.

"Medic," Cross said dryly.

"I just saw this!" Brighton finally managed to say. "It's real? Are we dealing with this?"

"Why is Brighton freaking out?" Walker asked.

"It's real," Cross replied to Brighton first. He addressed his next word to Walker and the others. "Watch."

At that, Cross tapped his touchscreen to start the video. The thrum of the snowmobiles' engines and the whistling of hard wind burst from the speakers in the briefing room. Cross tapped the touchscreen once more to mute the video.

"You're not missing anything without sound," he explained as the men in red rode through the snow. The camera bobbed and bounced with the motion of the snowmobile in the hands of the person carrying it. "These guys are geologists from Lost Aspen, an American mobile research station in Marie Byrd Land in western Antarctica. What they're up to here isn't relevant to our mission." He checked the screen and waited for a visual cue, then said, "But *this* is."

"And it's flippin' awesome!" Brighton added.

On the screen, the geologists started pointing and waving frantically. The lead snowmobile's passenger shook the shoulders of the driver, who then brought the snowmobile to a halt. The cameraman's driver stopped alongside them. More frantic gesturing from the first geologist made the rest look up to see what he was pointing at. The camera watched them for a few more seconds, then lurched around in a half circle and tilted skyward. Clouds wavered in and out of focus for a second before the cameraman found what the others had pointed at: a lance of white fire in the sky. The image focused, showing what appeared to be a meteorite, with a trailing white plume, punching through a hole in the clouds. The camera zoomed out to allow the cameraman to better track the meteorite's progress through the sky.

"Is that a meteorite?" Shepherd asked.

"Just keep watching," Brighton said.

Right on cue, the supposed meteorite suddenly flared white, then changed directions in mid-flight by almost 45 degrees. Grunts and hisses of surprise filled the room.

"So…not a meteorite," Shepherd muttered.

The members of Shadow Squadron watched in awe as the falling object changed direction once again, with another flare, and pitched downward. The camera angle twisted overhead and then lowered to track its earthward trajectory.

"And now…sonic boom," Brighton said.

The camera image shook violently as the compression

wave from the falling object broke the speed of sound. The accompanying burst made the cameraman's hands shake. A moment later, the object streaked into the distance and disappeared into the rolling hills of ice and snow. The video footage ended a few moments later with a still image of the geologists looking like a bunch of kids on Christmas morning.

"This video popped up on the Internet a few hours ago," Cross said. "It's already starting to go viral."

"What is it?" Jannati asked. "I can't imagine we'd get involved in this if it was just a meteor."

"Meteorite," Staff Sergeant Adam Paxton said. "If it gets through the atmosphere to the ground, it's a meteorite, not a meteor."

Brighton hopped out of his chair. "That wasn't a meteorite, man," he said. He dug his smartphone out of a pocket and came around the table toward the front of the room. He laid his phone on the touchscreen Cross had, then synced up the two devices. With that done, Brighton used his phone as a remote control to run the video backward to the first time the object had changed directions. He used a slider to move the timer back and forth, repeatedly showing the object's sharp angle of deflection through the sky.

"Meteorites can't change directions like this," Brighton said. "This is 45 degrees of deflection at least, and the thing barely even slows down. And it did it *twice*."

"I'm seeing a flare when it turns," Paxton said. "Meteors hold a lot of frozen water when they're in space, and it expands when it reaches the atmosphere. If those gases vented or exploded, couldn't that cause a change in direction?"

"Not this sharply," Brighton said before Cross could reply. "Besides, take a look at this." He used a few swipes across his phone to pause the video and zoom in on the flying object. At the new resolution, a dark oblong shape was visible inside a wreath of fire. He then advanced through the first and second changes of direction and tracked it a few seconds forward before pausing again. "See?"

A room full of shrugs and uncomprehending looks met Brighton's eager gaze.

Brighton tossed his hands up in mock frustration. "It's the same size!" he said. "If this thing had exploded twice — with enough force to push something this big in a different direction both times — it would be in a million pieces. So those aren't explosions. They're thrusters or ramjets or something."

"Which makes this what?" Shepherd asked. "A UFO?"

"Sure," Paxton answered in a mocking tone. "It's unidentified, it's flying, and it's surely an object."

"You don't know that it's *not* a UFO," Brighton said. "I mean, this thing could very well be from outer space!"

"Sit down, Sergeant," Chief Walker said.

Brighton reluctantly did so, pocketing his phone.

"Don't get ahead of yourself, Ed," Cross added, retaking control of the briefing. "Phantom Cell analysts have authenticated the video and concluded that this thing is some kind of metal construct, though they can't make out specifics from the quality of the video. I suppose it's possible it's from outer space, but it's much more likely it's man-made. The only thing we know for sure is that it isn't American-made. Therefore, our mission is to get out to where it came down, zip it up, and bring it back for a full analysis. Any questions?"

"I have one," Jannati said. "What is Phantom Cell?"

Cross nodded. As the newest member of the team, Jannati wasn't as familiar with the JSOC's various secret programs. "Phantom Cell is a parallel program to ours," Cross explained. "But their focus is on psy-ops, cyberwarfare, and research and development."

Jannati nodded. "Geeks, in other words," he said. Brighton gave him a sour look.

"What are we supposed to do about the scientists who found this thing?" Yamashita asked. True to his stoic and patient nature, the sniper had finished his breakfast and coffee while everyone else had been talking excitedly. "Do they know we're coming?"

Cross frowned. "That's the problem," he said. "We haven't heard a peep out of them since this video appeared online. Attempts at contacting them have gone unanswered. Last anyone heard, the geologists who made the video were going to try to find the point of impact where this object came down. We have no idea whether they found it or what happened to them."

"Isn't this how the movie *Aliens* started?" Brighton asked. "With a space colony suddenly cutting off communication after a UFO crash landing?"

Paxton rolled his eyes. "Lost Aspen's pretty new, and it's in the middle of Antarctica," he said. "It could just be a simple technical failure."

"You have zero imagination, man," Brighton said. "You're going to be the first one the monster eats. Well, after me, anyway." Some of the men laughed.

"These are our orders," Cross continued as if he had never been interrupted in the first place. "Locate the crashed object, bring it back for study, figure out why the research station stopped communicating, and make sure the civilians are safe. Stealth is going to be of paramount importance on this one. Nobody has any territorial claims on Marie Byrd Land, but no country is supposed to be sending troops on missions anywhere in Antarctica either."

"Are we expecting anyone else to be breaking that rule besides us, Commander?" Yamashita asked.

"It's possible," Cross said. "If this object is man-made, whoever made it is probably going to come looking for it. And any other government that attached the same significance to the video that ours did will send people, too. No specific intel has been confirmed yet, but we've heard whispers of Russian Special Forces on the scene."

"Seems like the longer the video's out there, the more likely we're going to have company," Yamashita said.

"About that," Cross said. "Phantom Cell's running a psy-ops campaign in support of our efforts. They're simultaneously spreading the word that the video's a hoax and doing their best to stop it from spreading any further."

"Good luck to them on that last one," Brighton said. "You can't stop the Internet. Phantom Cell's good, but nobody's *that* good."

"Not our concern," Cross said. "We ship out in one hour, so get your gear on the Commando. We'll go over more mission specifics during the flight. Understood?"

"Sir," the men responded in unison. At a nod from Cross, they rose and gathered up the remains of their breakfasts. As they left the briefing room, Walker remained behind. He gulped down the last of his coffee before standing up.

"Brighton's sure excited," Walker said.

"I knew he would be," Cross replied. "I didn't expect him to try to help out so much with the briefing, though."

Walker hesitated for a moment. "Is that what I'm like whenever I chip in from up here?" he asked.

Cross fought the urge to toy with his second-in-command, but he couldn't stop a mischievous smile from creeping across his face. "Maybe a little bit," he said.

Walker returned Cross's grin. "Then I wholeheartedly apologize," he said.

* * *

After several monotonous hours of flying in the MC130-J Commando II plane, Shadow Squadron made a single stop to transfer to a CH-53E Super Stallion transport helicopter. A few hours more, and the team was finally at its destination.

The blank, unbroken expanse of Marie Byrd Land, Antarctica, stretched out below. Half of the ground was obscured by cloud cover and glare from the sun.

As Cross peered down the horizon, he saw what looked like two parallel suns. "Am I hallucinating?" he asked, pointing at the strange sight.

Brighton answered him. "No, sir," he said. "That's a phantom sun. It's a phenomenon that occurs when sunlight is refracted through ice crystals. Pretty cool, if you ask me." Brighton nudged Yamashita in the ribs. "Kinda looks like a sniper scope's reticule, huh?"

"No," Yamashita answered flatly. He shot an annoyed look at Cross.

"I'm sorry I asked," Cross said with a chuckle. Brighton was usually pretty excitable on missions, but he seemed to be especially enthusiastic about this one.

As the Super Stallion began its descent, Cross clapped once to get his men's attention. "I know you've all been through Pickel Meadows and Kodiak and Black Rapids," he said, referring to the Marines', Navy's, and Army's respective northern and mountain training centers. "But this isn't going to be exactly like that. For one thing, it's actually summer right now in Antarctica. Temperatures could get up to a balmy

60 out on the coast — a little colder inland where we are. For another, it's not going to get dark. At all. The sun won't set down here for another month at least. That means you won't be able to rely on it for direction, either. Also, remember what Williams said about whiteout and snow blindness — keep your sunglasses on at all times when we're outdoors."

The helicopter thumped down hard onto the thickly packed Antarctic ice. Cross supervised his team's last-minute gear checks, then ordered the flight crew to lower the rear cargo hatch.

Frigid wind clawed its way into the cargo bay, easily overpowering the wall-mounted space heaters. Cross couldn't help but check to make sure everyone was properly bundled in their cold-weather gear.

"Lieutenant Commander?" Yamashita called, drawing Cross's attention back to the cargo ramp. The sniper stood at the top, facing down and outside toward something Cross couldn't see. His voice had the same tone of guarded caution Cross heard when Yamashita was waiting for the go-ahead to take a shot with his M110 rifle.

Cross walked over to Yamashita and found him staring at a stranger who stood midway up the ramp. His hands were out at both sides. He wasn't dressed in a military-issue, seven-layer Extended Cold Weather Clothing System (or ECWCS) like the members of Cross's team. Nor was he dressed like the airfield skeleton crew Cross could see coming toward the plane from farther off to refuel it. This man's winter gear was

all expensive, store-brand stuff that might as well have had the price tags still attached for how new it all looked.

Cross tilted his head as an introduction, wondering if the man was some civilian scientist who'd accidentally wandered into a place he shouldn't be.

"Lieutenant Commander Ryan Cross, I presume?" the stranger asked. He grinned. "Permission to come aboard, sir?"

"Who are you and what are you doing out here?" Cross demanded. The tone of the stranger's voice and the smug confidence in his grin reminded Cross of himself when he was much younger. It was an unpleasant mirror to gaze into.

"Bill Dyer," the man said. "From Phantom Cell. I've been assigned to your squadron for the duration of this mission."

"So you say," Cross replied. "How'd you get here so fast?" The men behind Cross read the tension in his body language and stopped to watch how things would play out.

Dyer's grin widened. "I was already on assignment not far from here," he said. "I hitched a ride with the ground crew."

"I'll have to confirm this with Command," Cross said.

"Sure, sure," Dyer said amiably.

Cross turned and headed back toward the helicopter's cockpit and gave Yamashita a look as he turned. Yamashita nodded his understanding and remained in Cross's place to glare at Dyer.

Picking up on the hint, Dyer strolled down the ramp and stood out of the way as Shadow Squadron continued to unload.

A quick call back to Command confirmed Dyer's story and earned Cross an apology for the slow communication from Phantom Cell. He informed his men of the change in plans and approached Dyer once more.

"You're legit," Cross said. "Sorry about that."

"No harm done," Dyer said, as if Cross hadn't kept him waiting. "And welcome to Pluto." That joke drew a chuckle from Brighton.

Cross looked around. The outpost where they'd landed extended into a blue-ice runway that continued for miles until it disappeared from sight. There were also two drab, pre-fabricated, semi-cylindrical buildings that were partially buried in snow and ice. They looked like giant cans that'd been dropped carelessly into the ground.

"Camp's not much to look at," Dyer said, noticing Cross's skepticism. "It's been abandoned for a few years since the Pine Island Glacier camp opened up. That one's a little more central and convenient to the stations that use it. We still had this place on record, though, and figured it would serve as a nice out-of-the-way base of operations. The ground crew cleaned the place out and got it up and running. In another few weeks, it might actually be warm in the main building. I wouldn't hold my breath, though."

Cross nodded for him to continue.

"The good news is," Dyer said, "I've been able to pinpoint the crash site you're here to find. It's only a dozen or so miles away, between us and Lost Aspen. I figure we should go ahead and check out the crash site first."

"How did you find it?" Brighton asked.

"It wasn't too hard," Dyer said with a cavalier smile. "I'm the one who caused the crash, after all."

Stunned silence followed that claim. Cross was the first to break it. "Come again?"

"Yeah, what is it?" Brighton asked.

"It's a hunter-killer drone satellite," Dyer explained. "Think of it like an orbital UAV. I caught it trying to hack into one of our spy satellites and engaged in a tug-of-war with its operator. I locked him out and stole it from him, but I couldn't keep it from crashing."

"Who built it?" Brighton asked.

"Probably the Chinese," Dyer said. "Regardless, the operator was definitely Chinese. I've crossed swords with him a few times, so to speak. I was able to blind him from where the drone crashed, so we've got a head start. But it's only going to be a matter of time before they figure that Internet video out and come looking. We need to get to the site in a hurry."

"All right," Cross said, annoyed with the way the Phantom Cell operative acted as if he were in charge. "As soon as the snowmobiles are ready and we get our gear set up, we'll head out there and check it out."

Dyer winced. "Actually, Commander, I was just coming to that," he said. "Snowmobiles might not be an option right now — unless you've got some of those Canadian stealth jobs."

"Canada has stealth snowmobiles?" Walker asked, his tone doubtful.

"Yeah, they're pretty cool, Chief," Brighton said. "They're hybrid-electric with like a 150-mile range. They can get up to, like, 50 miles per hour. I think they call them..." He looked back and forth between Walker and Cross, neither of whom seemed glad for his input. "Anyway, they're neat."

"Edgar Brighton," Dyer said, extending a hand. "It's a pleasure. Bill Dyer, Phantom Cell. We heard about what you did with the Avenger drone over Saraqeb. Impressive stuff."

"Thanks, man!" Brighton said, shaking Dyer's hand. If Brighton was at all disappointed to find that the object that had crashed wasn't an alien spaceship, he didn't show it. "Sounds kind of like what you did with this satellite drone thing."

Dyer winked. "Like I said, Impressive."

"What's this about the snowmobiles?" Cross cut in.

"We'll talk later, when you've got a minute," Dyer said to Brighton. To Cross, he said, "Silence is going to be golden on this one, Commander. The Chinese might not know where to look for their drone yet, but the Russians are already on the case. They landed a team a few hours before you got here."

"Are they scientists?" Chief Walker asked.

"Nope," Dyer said. "My information indicates they're Spetsnaz. I think they're responsible for the communications blackout from Lost Aspen. I don't have confirmation on that intel, though."

"Russian Special Forces," Cross said. "Could be worse, I guess. We're not technically enemies with them anymore."

"Just calling them Spetsnaz doesn't tell us much," Walker said. "You know anything more about the specific unit in play?"

Dyer shook his head. "Wish I did," he said. "But according to radio intercepts, they're definitely Russian and definitely here because of the video. They're ahead of us, but I can't say if they've found the site or not. They cut me off before I could learn more."

"Regardless, they're out there right now," Cross said. "Watching, listening, and with no more right to be here than we have. You're correct — we can't risk a noisy approach."

"Plus," Dyer added, "if they know that you know they're here, they'll go to great lengths to make sure you don't tell anybody. You know, since none of us should be here at all."

"Possibly," Walker said.

"You guys should consider alternatives," Dyer said. "I mean, as soon as they know we're here, it might be wise to —"

"No," Cross said. "That isn't how we operate. If operational security becomes a problem, we'll deal with it in due time. The Russians aren't my main concern, though — the scientists are. Making sure they are safe is our top priority."

"With all due respect, Commander," Dyer said, "the drone is the top priority."

"That's what it says on our orders," Cross said. "But I'm in charge here, and I decide what's most important. If you don't like that, you can take it up with Command."

"Duly noted," Dyer said neutrally.

"In any event," Cross continued, "the crash site is between us and Lost Aspen. We'll stop by there to see what we can see on the way. Got it?"

"I'm just an observer and technical advisor," Dyer said with a shrug. "You guys are the ones with the weapons. We'll do it your way."

"All right then," Cross said. He turned away to address his men. They quickly gathered around to listen. "We've confirmed there's a rival team on the field: Russian Special Forces — we don't know how many. They've got a head start, but we don't know how much of one. I don't need to remind you of the sticky legal situation our presence here represents. Suffice it to say, this operation just went from top-secret to full black. That means total noise discipline en route. We're leaving the snowmobiles behind and going out on the shorts. We'll recon the crash site and secure it if we're first on the scene, then radio back for the Super Stallion. I want you to finish unloading your gear, stretch your legs, change your socks, carb up, and hydrate. Then load up your ahkios because we're leaving in twenty minutes."

"Sir," the men responded.

When Cross finished, Dyer looked at him and pretended to cough behind his hand.

"Right, one more thing," Cross said. "This is Bill Dyer of Phantom Cell. He's coming with us as an advisor. He's the reason we're here, so I need a volunteer to buddy up and keep an eye on him."

"Can you ski?" Shepherd asked with a skeptical frown. "Or shoot? Did you even bring a gun?"

"Yes to all three," Dyer said. "My rifle's with the rest of my gear. And yeah, I can ski and shoot. I was an alternate on the '94 Olympic men's biathlon team."

Paxton smirked. "Didn't the Russians take home the most gold medals in biathlon that year?" he asked.

"Only because I didn't get to compete against them," Dyer assured him.

"Thank you for volunteering, Sergeant," Cross said to Paxton. "Make sure Dyer and his gear are ready to go when we are."

"Sir," Paxton said.

"Twenty minutes, people," Cross reiterated to the whole team. "Get started."

* * *

The first leg of Shadow Squadron's journey to the crash site proceeded without incident. The team set out on their ski-shoes, which combined the best features of skis and snowshoes.

The carbon fiber ski-shoes offered a wide, flat base for moving over loose powder or uphill. They also had a set of corrugated scales beneath the soles of the soldiers' boots, which offered traction without inhibiting forward motion.

Dyer was outfitted similarly, but once again his equipment was top-of-the-line professional sports gear rather than the field-tested special order equipment Shadow Squadron soldiers used.

As they traveled, the soldiers wore their seven-layer ECWCS outfits with digital white-blue-gray camouflage. They carried their rifles on their backs. The rest of their gear they dragged behind them in lightweight carbon fiber ahkio sleds attached to harnesses on their belts. The only exception in this case was Dyer, who had only brought a heavy backpack and had no sled.

The sun and its double looped through the sky, flirting with the horizon but never quite touching it. Cross resisted the urge to go all the way to the crash site immediately. He was concerned that the lack of a regular day-and-night cycle would cause him to accidentally push his men too hard and wear them out early. When his compass and GPS told him the team was still a couple of miles from the crash site, he ordered them to stop and make camp.

The men dug down several feet through the ice and snow and set up tents along with an electric field stove. Then the team ate and took turns resting for the long trip to follow.

Although Dyer had stayed by Paxton's side for the whole

trip thus far, Cross noticed that the Phantom Cell operative had barely said a word to Paxton once camp was set up. Instead, Dyer spent most of his time talking to Brighton, praising the short-range Four-Eyes UAV drone that Brighton had designed. Then he went on to engage him in a discussion of computing and surveillance technology that sounded more like science fiction to Cross than anything with real-world applications. Then again, Cross hadn't been able to imagine anything like smartphones or UAV drones when he'd first joined the Navy. Now those things were everywhere.

Since the pair of them were getting along so well, Cross reassigned Brighton to keep an eye on Dyer, which suited both men just fine. Paxton privately admitted to being relieved after Cross informed him of the switch. Paxton couldn't explain exactly why, but something about Dyer rubbed him the wrong way. Cross didn't respond to Paxton's concern, but his impression of Dyer was similar. The man had an air of competence and charisma about him, but it was an oily sort of charisma. A youthful kind of cockiness that flew in the face of caution for the sake of success.

"That could be it," Chief Walker said after Cross expressed his concerns. "Or it could be you're just getting old, Commander. Same stuff comes to mind when I think about you most days." Walker tried to hide his smirk behind his tin coffee cup.

"I see," Cross said. "Thanks for that, Chief."

"Anytime, sir."

Some hours later, the soldiers broke camp and set out in silence once again. They made remarkable time, moving primarily downhill over smooth terrain. Well before lunchtime, they topped a small hill, which gave them their first view of the site where the drone had crashed.

Cross called everyone to a stop. The men gathered up around him. "This is the place," he said. "And it's right where you said it would be, Dyer. Good work."

"Math," Dyer replied with a shrug of humility. Cross didn't buy it.

The site itself wasn't all that impressive. The impact crater was comet-shaped where the drone had come in at a shallow angle. It had melted a trail and gouged a hole in the frozen landscape. Cottony diamond dust settled low over the area, making the air sparkle.

"Binoculars," Cross said. "Glass and FLIR. Let's take a look around before we get down there."

The soldiers drew their ahkios in close and kneeled over their ski-shoes to examine the crash site with regular field binoculars and forward-looking infrared (or FLIR) binoculars. Dyer got down beside Brighton and scanned the area with a single-lens FLIR spyglass.

Yamashita kicked out of his ski-shoes to lie prone at the crest of the hill. He lay looking casually over the area with the Leupold scope on his M110 sniper rifle. A taut mesh of loose-weave white nylon covered the end of his scope, though it didn't seem to obscure his vision.

"No wreckage," Yamashita said.

"No scientists, either," Walker added, peering through one of the sets of FLIR binoculars. "Or Russians."

"I see tracks," Cross said. "Snowmobile tracks back and forth on the far side. The ones leading out have a heavy trench behind and between them. They don't look that fresh. Probably from the geologists. There are ski tracks too that come in from a different angle. Looks like they head off in the direction the snowmobiles came from. They're fresher, too."

"They're probably from the Russians," Walker said. "Tracking the geologists."

"*Hunting* them," Dyer corrected.

"If my read's right," Cross said, "the scientists in the video found this site, attached the drone to their snowmobiles, and then dragged it back to Lost Aspen. Sometime later, the Russians showed up and followed the trail back. They could be at Lost Aspen already."

"They almost certainly are," Dyer said. "It's time to consider a full —"

Cross was about to set Dyer straight on who was giving the orders when the ground several feet down the hill in front of them suddenly sprayed snow into the air.

Cross flinched and watched the tiny white flakes drift back to earth.

"What the heck?" Dyer asked, looking just as surprised as Cross felt.

Another puff of snow shot up in front of Walker's feet. "Sniper!" Yamashita hissed, figuring it out at the same time Cross did. "Find cover!"

Cross and Walker dove backward, hoping to put the crest of their small hill between themselves and the shooter. Brighton, meanwhile, lurched out of his ski-shoes to tackle Dyer to the ground.

A sharp noise broke the eerie silence of the attack. Both Brighton and Dyer yelped in surprise and pain as they landed in a tangle of arms and legs and rolled down the hill, bumping awkwardly over Dyer's bulky backpack. Williams, the team's medic, popped out of his ski-shoes and crawl-slid over to them to check for injuries.

"Sleds up!" Cross ordered, yanking his ahkio up beside him where he lay, hauling it one-handed toward the hilltop.

The others began to do the same, balancing their sleds on edge in the snow, using the weight of the gear strapped on top of the sleds to keep them balanced upright. They lined up the ahkios in a crooked line that looked like the tops of a medieval castle wall, then they hunkered down behind them. The advanced carbon fiber skin over the lightweight metal core of the sleds made them somewhat bullet resistant, if not bulletproof. In any case, the sleds offered better cover than the snowy nothingness all around them.

With the quick-and-dirty wall erected, Cross motioned for the others to move back down the hill away from it and slide over to the left. While he'd seen video of the sleds stopping small-arms fire, he didn't want to test his luck against a high-powered sniper rifle. He also didn't want the sniper to get lucky by arcing his shots over the makeshift wall. When the others were relocated, only Yamashita remained on the line, lying exactly where he'd been the whole time. He hadn't flinched at the signs of gunfire, nor had he moved his sled into line with the others. He just lay perfectly still, looking downrange through his Leupold scope with the patience of a stone.

Cross came to check on Brighton and Dyer. "They're all right, Commander," Williams said. "No blood, no foul. Neither one of them was hit."

"That jerk blew up my binoculars," Brighton said. He sat up and showed Cross the remains of the black-and-gray FLIR lenses. They had been dangling around his neck from a long nylon lanyard when he'd tackled Dyer to pull him to safety. The binoculars now had a small hole on one side where the bullet had gone in and an enormous blossom of twisted metal and plastic on the other side where the bullet had exited.

"I swear to you, he will pay for that," Dyer said with all the charisma of a Shakespearean actor. "He. Will. Pay."

Brighton snickered and punched Dyer in the shoulder.

"Stay down," Cross told the two of them. To Williams he said, "Which one of the sleds is yours?"

"Far left," Williams said, nodding at the sled closest to Yamashita. "Why?"

"Could be important," Cross said. "I just hope it isn't."

Without further explanation, Cross crawled back up the hill to the ahkio wall and opened Williams' gear. He dug out a medical bag and slid it back down the hill to where the medic lay waiting. Next, he picked up a pair of FLIR binoculars and edged toward the first gap in the sled wall, hoping to determine where the enemy sniper was hiding.

"Don't," Yamashita said calmly. "He'll see the glare."

He's right, Cross realized. The sun was behind the opposing sniper, shining in Cross's eyes. In fact, it was so bitterly cold and clear that phantom suns shone to the right and left of the actual sun, giving the entire landscape the look of an alien planet. Thanks to Brighton's excited explanation earlier, Cross now knew that the phantom suns were just optical illusions created by ice crystals. But that fact didn't make the sight seem any less creepy under the circumstances.

Regardless, the light was more than bright enough to cast a glare off the lenses of his binoculars and give his position away. Fortunately, the nylon mesh over the end of Yamashita's rifle scope prevented that from happening to him.

"Do you see him?" Cross whispered to Yamashita.

"I haven't fired yet, sir," Yamashita replied. "I've got eyes on a couple of likely spots, but he hasn't obliged me by moving or shooting again."

"Think we can slip behind where you think he is?" Cross asked.

"Not if he's any good," Yamashita said.

"If he were any good, he would have hit at least one of us with those first three shots," Cross argued.

"That wasn't for lack of skill," Yamashita said. "It's a problem with optics in terrain like this. Things in the distance look bigger and closer than they really are since everything is one color. It just took him a couple of shots to adjust for difference. The fact he didn't get a kill on his third shot was pure dumb luck."

"I see," Cross said, unsettled by the close call. "This is your game. What's our next move?"

"If you can get him to shoot again without getting yourself killed, I'll take it from there, Commander," Yamashita said. He paused for a second and then added, "Well, either way... When he shoots, I will take him out."

"My soul will rest easy knowing that," Cross murmured. "Okay, hang tight. I've got an idea."

Moving carefully and hoping not to draw the enemy sniper's attention, Cross picked up the binoculars he'd been about to use. Then he rolled as fast as he could across the first gap in the sled wall to where the next two sleds sat end to end. His heart raced, fearing that the sniper would see the sudden motion and put a one-in-a-million shot through the gap. When no shot came, his heart kept racing, anyway. Cross also feared that the sniper saw the roll but was just patiently lining up a kill shot that would punch through the shield wall and into him.

After another few eternally long, pulse-pounding seconds, Cross's fears finally dimmed. Pulling his fur-lined cap off from beneath his jacket's hood, Cross laid it down on top of the binoculars he'd grabbed. These he laid on the curved underside of one of the ski-shoes Paxton had kicked off when the warning had gone out. Then, lying on his back behind the first of the two adjacent sleds, he used the ski-shoe to lift the hat and binoculars ever-so-slowly up over the top edge of the second sled. When it was just high enough, he propped it up on the side of the sled. His hope was that the lenses of the binoculars would cast a glare and attract the enemy sniper's attention, and that the silhouette of the hat and binoculars would look like a soldier peering up over the top of the —

CRACK! At first, Cross didn't realize what had happened. One second he was looking up at his decoy and wondering how long it would take for the sniper to take the bait. A split-second later, the binoculars exploded. The hat went flying and a piece of the binoculars snapped off and flew past Cross's face, nicking his cheek.

At what seemed like the same instant, a muted cough came from Yamashita's rifle. A second later, the sickening sound of impact came back from the opposite end of the crash site.

"Clear," Yamashita said. His voice was quiet and subdued, but he didn't whisper.

Cross pressed a hand to his cheek. His mitten came away with a thin, short line of blood from where the bit of shrapnel had cut him. "You sure you got him?"

Yamashita gave a small shudder that only Cross was close enough to see. "I have eyes on the target now, Commander," he said. "I got him." He said the last three words so quietly they almost disappeared in the icy wind.

Cross knew Yamashita well enough to know better than to the praise the quality of his shooting. "Does he have a spotter?" Cross asked.

"No," Yamashita replied.

"Must have been a sentry," Cross speculated. "Probably radioed in as soon as he saw us."

"I would have," Yamashita agreed.

Cross frowned. "That means either reinforcements are coming, or they're going to be holed up waiting for us when we get to Lost Aspen."

"Either way, we don't have much time to wait around, sir," Yamashita said.

Cross nodded. "Gear up and get your short-skis back on. Take your partner and head up the path. Scout the way and find out what you can. We'll join you shortly."

"Sir," Yamashita said. He waved downhill to get Jannati's attention and signaled the Marine to join him. They paired up and Yamashita explained Cross's orders. Jannati nodded and got his gear together.

Cross descended the hill to address the remaining men. "Sniper's down," he began, "but it's more than likely the enemy knows we're here and figures we're on the way. They're either going to meet us halfway or dig in and let us come to them."

"And they're probably going to start executing the civilians," Dyer said under his breath. "So there are no witnesses."

"You'll speak when I ask for your opinion," Cross snapped at him.

Dyer flinched. "Sir, yessir," he drawled. His tone was low and flippant, but he broke eye contact under the force of Cross's glare.

"Gear up," Cross said to his men. "We're moving out."

* * *

To give Yamashita and Jannati time to move ahead and scout, Cross led his men over to the dead Russian sniper for a quick examination. What was left of him wasn't very helpful. The man carried no ID papers or personal mementos. The only equipment he had was a pack of energy bars, a two-way earpiece radio, a VSS Vintorez sniper rifle, and half a dozen magazines for his weapon.

Only Cross had the stomach to remove the sniper's earpiece and dig the radio out of his coat. He looped the earpiece over his ear, opposite the one in which his own canalphone nestled. A double-pop of static indicated a signal from the sniper's comrades. Cross repeated the signal with taps on the transmitting part of the earpiece. One more pop came over the line, then a wary Russian voice spoke a single phrase.

Without pressing the earpiece to transmit, Cross looked at Walker. "Sub-shot?" he asked, repeating the Russian he'd heard as best he could repeat it. "What's that mean, Chief? Or it might have been sub-shet…"

"Report," Walker replied.

When Cross didn't answer, the voice spoke again.

"Sh-toe shloo-chee-less?" Cross relayed. "K-toe ah-nee?"

"'What happened?' maybe," Walker said. "Then, 'Who are they?' Sir, if you want me to try to talk to —"

"I've got it," Cross said.

After a long pause, Cross still didn't reply. In response, the radio clicked one more time and then fell silent. Cross cocked an eyebrow in thought, feeling every eye on him. He looked at Walker, then at Dyer before he spoke.

"How many people are stationed at Lost Aspen?" he asked.

"Forty-one," Dyer said. "Assuming your Spetsnaz counterparts haven't —"

Cross cut Dyer off with a hard glare. Then he tapped the dead Russian's radio earpiece, opening the channel.

"I know you can hear me," Cross said softly into the radio. "You and I need to talk. Sooner rather than later."

"What are you doing?" Dyer hissed. His eyes widened so much that his eyebrows completely cleared the tops of his expensive mirrored shades.

"Sir…" Walker said.

"Kto eto?" a flat voice said from the other end of the Russian radio frequency. It wasn't the same one that had spoken before.

"I'm going to assume," Cross said, "that you just asked me either who I am or what I want. Is that right?"

"Da," the Russian replied. Then under a heavy accent, "Yes, the first. Who are you?"

"Does it matter?" Cross asked.

"Nyet. Not really."

"So ask me what you really want to know."

"My soldier," the Russian said. "You have him?"

"No," Cross said. "He fired on us. He's dead."

The Russian made no reply for almost a minute. Cross desperately hoped the man was simply composing himself rather than ordering his men to start executing scientists. When he finally spoke again, his voice was as flat and emotionless as before. "You have any casualties?"

"No," Cross said.

"How many men are with you?" he asked.

Cross smirked. "Enough to get the job done. You?"

"More than plenty," the Russian said. "Though now one less."

"Let me bring you his remains," Cross said, causing Walker and Dyer to flinch in surprise. "This is no fit place for a soldier to rest."

"That's…an unexpected offer," the voice said. "You would do this?"

"Yes," Cross said. "In exchange for a chance to talk."

"And what have we to talk about?" he asked.

"I'd say we have 41 things left yet to talk about," Cross said. "Or 42, if you count the real reason we were both sent here."

"Indeed," the Russian said. "Very well. Bring the body to the end of the trail. We will speak there, you and I. Only you and I."

"Understood," Cross said. "Out."

He tapped the Russian earpiece one last time and removed it from his ear. Before Walker or Dyer could start in on him, Cross double-tapped his own canalphone.

"Commander?" Yamashita replied, his voice barely above a whisper.

"I take it you're in position," Cross said. "You have eyes on Lost Aspen?"

"Sir."

"Any sign of the scientists?"

"Not unless they use assault rifles in their research,"

Yamashita said. "If they do, then I count nine 'scientists.' Four on top of the station, two at the main door of the flag-section — that'll make sense when you see this place — and three standing guard over something wrapped up tight in white tarps. Probably the drone. Orders, sir?"

"Hang tight and don't give yourselves away," Cross said. "We're going to move up in a few minutes, then I'm going down to Lost Aspen alone to have a chat."

"Sir," Yamashita replied.

Cross turned to address the rest of Shadow Squadron as they gathered around him. "All right, here's what I want you all to do…"

* * *

It took Cross only a few minutes to unload his ahkio then wrap and place the dead Russian sniper on it. But in that time, he got an earful from both Walker and Dyer about his plan. Walker was at least respectful enough to keep his opinion pitched low so the rest of the men didn't hear, but Dyer objected loudly and repeatedly. Neither of them could see what Cross hoped to gain by going into the lion's den alone, even if the rest of the team was watching in silence from nearby. While Cross respected Walker's opinion, it didn't help the Chief's case that Dyer agreed with him.

But Cross was determined to take the route he'd chosen. So once the rest of the team had moved up without him, Cross came sliding up to Lost Aspen all alone, pulling a corpse on a sled behind him.

Cross noticed that Lost Aspen itself was gorgeous. Based on a group of British architects' brilliant design plans, the facility resembled an enormous metal centipede on skis. It consisted of several house-sized modules rising over 20 feet off the snow on sets of hydraulic struts functioning as broad-flat skis. Each module connected to the one behind by way of a flexible, accordion-like hallway. Six of the modules were painted glossy green. The center module was the largest of the seven, and it had been painted in a wrap-around American flag. Cross had read about the British Halley VI Antarctic Research Station on which the design of Lost Aspen had been modeled. If the designs were as similar as they looked, that meant the flag section was the communal and entertainment center for the facility.

Two guards stood posted by the main door of the flag section, just as Yamashita had reported. A quick glance around revealed seven more sentinels more or less where he had expected them. These soldiers wore layered cold-weather gear. They carried AN-94 assault rifles, and their faces were obscured by ski masks.

Two soldiers waited beside the tarp-wrapped remains of the downed orbital drone. Cross spared it a glance before turning his attention to the lone figure who approached him across the ice on cleated boots.

"Here we go," Cross murmured, barely moving his lips. The comm channel remained open through the canalphone in his ear.

The Russian stopped ten feet from Cross and looked him over, his rifle in his hands but aimed at nothing. Unlike the others, he had taken his mask off. His face was hard-set and lined. His eyes were shimmering with equal parts caution and cunning. He made no effort to hide his suspicion.

"You are he?" the Russian said. Cross recognized the man's voice from the radio.

Cross nodded. He gestured at the ahkio behind him. "I am. And I've brought your man."

The Russian stepped forward and extended a gloved hand, keeping his other hand on his rifle. "Give me the lead," he said.

"First let's talk about what you've got under that tarp," Cross said.

"The satellite?" the Russian said. He gestured at the science facility behind him. "Perhaps you want to talk about what's wrapped inside that garish flag first."

Cross caught his meaning and nodded. "Yes, the scientists," he said. "They're American citizens."

"As are you, I think," the Russian said. "Unless that's a Canadian accent I am hearing."

"They're civilians," Cross said. "They've got nothing to do with this. Out of all of us, they're the only ones with any right to be here."

The Russian cocked his head and peered at Cross stone-faced. "Ask me what you really want to know."

"Are they dead?" Cross asked flatly.

"No."

Cross was barely able to conceal his surprise. "No? Then what are your intentions toward them?"

"I was prepared to live and let live," the Russian replied. "They need never have known we were here."

This time, Cross couldn't hide his surprise. "Come again?" he asked.

"We incapacitated them with a sleeping agent administered through the ventilation system," the Russian said.

"Like in the Dubrovka theater?" Cross asked, his blood running cold. Spetsnaz soldiers had used a similar tactic some years ago to subdue terrorists who'd taken a theater full of civilians hostage in Moscow. While the terrorists had been defeated once the gas took effect, more than 100 hostages died from adverse reactions to that gas.

The Russian scowled. "That was the work of thugs," he said. "No finesse. Besides, that was a decade ago." He took a deep breath, and his face returned to its neutral expression. "No, right now, the biggest risk to these people's safety is you and your men."

"How do you figure?" Cross asked.

"It is my understanding that your military does not negotiate over hostages in situations such as this," he said. "Especially not on your illegal 'black ops,' yes?"

"That's not my policy," Cross said. "Personally I don't care what's under that tarp. I want to know my people are all right. I'll do whatever it takes to make sure of it."

The Russian blinked in surprise. "You are not here for the satellite, then?" he said.

"It's a secondary objective," Cross said. "Frankly, if what you're saying is true, you can walk away with the satellite right now."

"Then I assure you it is true," the Russian said. His words rolled out slowly, as if his mind couldn't process what Cross said. "You have my word."

Cross smirked. "Give me some credit for common sense. What's that old saying? 'Trust but verify.'"

The Russian cracked a smile. "As you wish. If you will come with me..."

"I'll just wait here, thanks," Cross said. He turned his head to the side and said, "All right, Sergeant. Four Eyes is a 'go.' Check things out in the middle section of the facility."

Cross turned his attention back to the Russian. "Tell your men to leave the door open," he said.

At Cross's order, Brighton remotely activated the Four Eyes UAV quad-copter that had sat unnoticed on the ahkio sled between the dead sniper's boots. The UAV hummed to life and rose to shoulder height behind Cross.

"Sir," Brighton said over Cross's canalphone.

"Krúto," the Russian murmured with an impressed look on his face.

"It's just a camera platform," Cross said as the UAV buzzed past him and began to slowly move toward Lost Aspen. "No weapons, no explosives."

The Russian ordered the guards at the flag module to open the doors, and one of them went inside with the UAV. Several long moments later, Brighton's voice sounded in Cross's canalphone.

"All the civilians are accounted for, sir," Brighton said. "Looks like they're all sleeping."

"Sir," Williams cut in. "They're all alive and they appear to be unconscious. I can't say more without a proper examination, but it looks like they're all right."

"Okay," Cross said, both to his men and to the Russian. "I'm satisfied."

The Russian nodded. Brighton piloted the UAV back out of the flag module and landed it next to Cross.

"All right," Cross said. "If you and your men are willing to leave without giving us any trouble, you can take your prize and go. I'll be happy to remember we never saw you."

"And we likewise," the Russian said. His tone and expression remained wary, as if he believed he was being tricked. "Now, if I may…"

Once more, he extended a hand, palm up, reaching for

the lead to the ahkio sled with his comrade's body on it. This time, Cross met him halfway and handed the lead over.

The Russian pulled the sled over to him and knelt beside it. He grabbed a corner of the covering Cross had used as a shroud. After a brief hesitation, he peeled it back. The man winced at the condition of the body that lay revealed. The Russian's shoulders sagged for a moment, but he was all business by the time he covered his fallen comrade and stood to face Cross once again.

"We didn't expect anyone else to get here so quickly," the Russian said, staring out at the endless white horizon. "I only ordered him to watch over the crash site to get him out of my hair for a while." He sighed, and his eyes focused on Cross's once more. "Thank you for bringing him back."

Cross gave no reply. There was nothing he could say that the Russian would have wanted to hear.

"Now, we have preparations to make. Our Mi-8 will be here within the hour. I suggest you withdraw to wherever the rest of your men are hiding until we are gone. I do not want to have to explain your presence." He glanced down at the ahkio again. "I suspect I shall have more than enough to answer for."

"You and me both, Comrade," Cross said.

* * *

Cross and his team regrouped at Lost Aspen. Williams, Chief Walker, and Paxton were looking after the scientists now that they'd regained consciousness. No one seemed to be suffering any ill effects from whatever chemical the Russians had used on them, but a fleet of rescue helicopters had been called in to evacuate everyone as a precaution.

In the meantime, the scientists were starting to ask questions. Dyer set to work, feeding them the simple cover story he'd made up. According to him, the US military had sent in the Marines to investigate after communication with the research station had suddenly ceased. The soldiers had found everyone sleeping peacefully in the facility with no indication of what had happened to them. He pretended to be completely confused when they asked questions about the strange object they had recovered from the meteorite crash site. He repeated over and over that there was no evidence of any such object nearby.

When the scientists grew more insistent, Dyer simply asked them about the object. He knew full-well that none of them could tell him anything specific about it since even the four scientists from the video who'd recovered it had only a vague idea of what it was. They knew it was metal and that it was man-made. Beyond that, they couldn't recall anything. And the more Dyer questioned them and worked them over, the less certain they became of the object's existence.

Cross had to admit that Dyer was good at his job. By confusing their memories of the event, he'd made their claims too insufficient for even a conspiracy theory.

After the last of the scientists were evacuated, Dyer had a brief conversation with Brighton, then left. Cross was debating the best way to ask about the discussion when Brighton decided to approach him.

"I can't believe you just gave that device to the Russians, man," Brighton said.

"Command's not going to be happy," Cross admitted, "but I stand by my decision. I'd do it again if given the same opportunity."

"Well, sure, but what if it had been something from outer space?" Brighton asked. "I mean, baby Superman could've been in there, and now he'd be Russian, thanks to you."

Cross chuckled. "That's why I keep you around, Sergeant. I value your pragmatic, grounded sense of perspective."

Cross had expected a laugh from Brighton, but the Combat Controller's expression clouded over. "Now that you mention it," he said, "there's something I need to talk to you about." He paused for a moment. "Dyer offered me a job."

Cross wasn't surprised. Dyer's interest in Brighton had been obvious from the start. "With Phantom Cell, I take it?" Cross asked.

"Yeah," Brighton said, staring at his boots. "Apparently part of the reason they sent him out with us was to evaluate how I operate in the field. Did you know about this?"

"First I've heard of it," Cross said. A half-smile tugged at the side of his mouth. "You didn't really have to do much this time out, though, did you?"

"I saved Dyer's life," Brighton said. "As it turns out, that goes a long way in a job interview."

Cross grew serious. "Are you going to take his offer?"

"I don't know," Brighton said. "Should I? I'm qualified. I can do the work — probably better than anybody I know. It's a different kind of work, though. What do you think?"

Cross considered his response carefully. "I think Phantom Cell operates very differently than we do. Remember what Dyer kept obsessing about? The drone, the drone, the drone. He didn't care about the civilians. He certainly didn't care about the Russians. I'm sure he would've just as soon let us storm this place and kill as many 'enemy combatants' as we could in order to get that drone away from them. But it's like I told him before: that's not how we operate. If Phantom Cell *does* operate that way…is that something that you want to be a part of?"

"They might not all be like that," Brighton said without much conviction. "But even if they are, I'm not. Maybe I can change things for the better."

"If anyone could, it'd be you," Cross agreed. "In any case, I can't make this decision for you, and it's not one you should be in a hurry to make for yourself. Give yourself time to think through all the possibilities. Just make sure you do what's best for you."

"All right, Commander," Brighton said with a frown. "I'll let you know what I decide to do."

As Brighton walked away, Cross put his back to Lost Aspen and looked up at the sky. The phantom sun's light cast a weak, gloomy pall over everything. The South Pole's summer was almost over, and the cold winds hinted at a long winter still to come.

A shiver went up his spine — one that had nothing to do with the Antarctic cold.

MISSION DEBRIEFING

OPERATION

PHANTOM SUN 5678

MISSION COMPLETE

PRIMARY OBJECTIVE

x Locate & secure crashed aircraft

- Maintain anonymity

SECONDARY OBJECTIVES

- Avoid hostilities with Russian
  forces

STATUS

2/3 COMPLETE

3245.98 ● ● ●

CROSS, RYAN

RANK: Lieutenant Commander
BRANCH: Navy SEAL
PSYCH PROFILE: Team leader
of Shadow Squadron. Control
oriented and loyal, Cross insisted
on hand-picking each member of
his squad.

Our primary objective was to secure the crashed aircraft, but I refuse to believe that any piece of technology is worth risking forty-plus American lives, let alone waging war with Russian Special Forces. To my mind, we came away from this mission losing nothing except, possibly, a Combat Controller.

I have to admit that the thought of losing Brighton is unnerving. It would be hard -- maybe impossible -- to find a better man for the job...

– Lieutenant Commander Ryan Cross

2019.681

MISSION BRIEFING

OPERATION

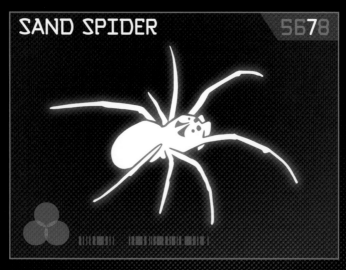

SAND SPIDER 5678

I've received an urgent call from a senator involved with Shadow Squadron's budget. To say he has a request is not entirely accurate -- it's more like a demand. In any event, if we want to keep receiving funding for the team, we have to head to Mali and rescue his kidnapped son.

I expect the team's cooperation to be top-notch after we finish extensive cohesion training with our new combat controller, Morgan Lancaster.

- Lieutenant Commander Ryan Cross

3245.98

MALI

PRIMARY OBJECTIVES

- Determine location of hostage

- Escort hostage to safety

SECONDARY OBJECTIVES

- Avoid conflict with local forces

1932.789

0412.981

1624.054

1324.014

SAND SPIDER

Lieutenant Commander Ryan Cross assembled his men in the briefing room as early as he dared, considering the previous evening's festivities. They'd held a going-away party for Edgar Brighton, the team's former combat controller. Brighton had been a member of the team since its creation, but he'd accepted his reassignment offer from Phantom Cell. From now on, he'd work for the highly classified psy-ops and cyber warfare division of the Department of Defense that promised to make better use of his intellect and technical skills.

That left Cross with a hole to fill in his team. A rather big one, since Brighton was excellent at his job. But after a long period of paperwork evaluations and a handful of interviews, Cross was finally ready to introduce Brighton's replacement to the rest of the team.

As usual, Walker arrived in the room first, followed closely by the five remaining soldiers of Cross's team. Except for Sergeant Shepherd, none of them looked worse for the wear from their partying the night before. Shepherd, however, was sporting a black eye from his ride on a mechanical bull at Brighton's going-away party. All of them sat quietly and glanced at the empty chair at the middle of the table. Brighton's absence was sorely felt.

"Let's get started," Cross said. He clicked on a touchpad built into the tabletop. The projector in the ceiling displayed the globe-and-crossed-swords emblem of Joint Special Operations Command on the whiteboard behind him. "With Staff Sergeant Brighton having moved on, we need to train his replacement and get the team back up to full cohesion."

The men nodded. When Shadow Squadron was created, the men had to go through nearly a year of special cohesion training. The purpose was to blend a group of individuals with different skills and military backgrounds into a functioning, singular unit. When Jannati arrived from the Marines Special Operations Regiment to replace the deceased Larssen, another month and a half of the same training was required to integrate him into the team. Now with the arrival of Brighton's replacement, another period of more cohesion training lay ahead of them.

Shepherd spoke up first. "So who's the new guy? And when's he getting here?"

Cross grinned. "Now," he said. He tapped a button next to the touchpad on the table, keying an intercom. "Send Lancaster in," he said in the intercom microphone's direction.

"Sir," came the reply from a nearby speaker.

As the door opened, all the men turned in expectation. The newest member of Shadow Squadron entered the room.

"Gentlemen," Cross said, "this is Staff Sergeant Morgan Lancaster, US Air Force Combat Controller."

"Morning," Sergeant Lancaster said. She closed the door behind her and waited. For what seemed like a long time, no one spoke or moved. Cross waited to see how his men would react to his choice. As he'd privately hoped, it was Shepherd who broke the silence.

"A girl," Shepherd said. He stood up and crossed over to stand in front of her. The top of Lancaster's head came up even with Shepherd's Adam's apple, so when he stopped she had to look up at him. "I thought you'd be, um...prettier."

Anger flashed in Chief Walker's face. He leaned forward and opened his mouth to say something, but Cross stopped him with a glance and a subtle wave of his hand. Walker remained silent despite his obvious frustration.

"I beg your pardon?" Lancaster said to Shepherd.

"You know, like if you have to distract a guard with your pretty smile," Shepherd went on, as if what he was saying was completely reasonable. "Or if you have to infiltrate a high class society function in a fancy evening dress. You look way too tough to do any of that, if you ask me."

Lancaster let a hint of a smile play around the corner of her mouth. "Hello, Mark. It's good to see you haven't changed at all."

Shepherd dropped the act and broke out in a huge grin. They shook hands. "Hey, Morgan," he said. "It's been a long time. How's your sister doing?"

"Better off," Lancaster said. Her grin was bigger than Shepherd's now.

Walker relaxed a little. "So you two know each other."

"Yeah, Chief," Shepherd said, looking over his shoulder at Walker. "We went to high school together. I dated her sister." Shepherd noticed the growing impatience on Cross's face. "Sorry about that, Commander. Just caught me a little off guard is all."

"No harm done," Cross said. To Lancaster he said, "Welcome, Sergeant. Have a seat."

"Thank you, Sir," Lancaster said.

To bring the team up to speed, Cross laid out a brief overview of Lancaster's background and qualifications. According to his research and interviews, Lancaster had joined the Air Force just before the Pentagon had removed the ban on women serving in combat roles in the US military. The ban had been an official Department of Defense rule since only the mid-1990s despite being an ongoing military tradition long before that. But with the most recent wars in Iraq and Afghanistan, women in supposedly non-combat roles were being put in exactly the same danger as their male fellow-soldiers. After a time, it became clear just how senseless and sexist the rule had been.

When the Secretary of Defense lifted the restriction, Lancaster was among the first wave of women who sought to push even further into the male-only special operations sector. While most of the military engaged in endless debates and bureaucratic foot-dragging, the Air Force's Combat Control quietly opened its admissions to women who were willing to meet its program's high physical and mental standards. Lancaster had been one of the select few women who made it all the way from the Combat Control Selection Course to Combat Control School. In short order, she earned her level-three ranking as a combat controller.

Afterward, Lancaster was ushered through the Special Tactics Advanced Skills Training courses. She quickly learned free-fall parachuting and combat diving, among other specialized skills. Throughout the process, she earned some of the best scores and ratings in the past decade. Some of her scores were even better than Brighton's had been.

Cross described Lancaster's recent deployments and the medals she had won for her exemplary service. What he left out, however, was a revelation Lancaster had made in her last interview: being part of his team was not her ideal career move. Were it up to her, she would have continued her training until she became the Air Force's first female officer — not just an operative.

In other words, she wants my job, Cross thought. And he couldn't blame her for her frustration. As progressive as the Air Force had been thus far, Lancaster found her progress stifled. The process of selection at the Special Tactics Officer level was a series of interviews with older, long-serving officers. Sadly, none of them had shown the slightest interest in considering her for the officer program. While it was easier for the Air Force to move forward with integrating its male and female combatants, expecting the same progressive attitude from every individual was a dream yet to be realized.

All the same, Lancaster gladly accepted Cross's offer to join the team. Her sense of duty, Cross had come to realize, was greater than her specific career aspirations. The team needed her exceptional skills and dedication. And after all, Shadow Squadron did valuable work outside the cumbersome restrictions of the greater military bureaucracy. To Cross, it didn't matter whether that work was done by a man or woman as long as the soldier in question was skilled enough to get the job done. Lancaster was that sort of soldier, Cross believed.

"Welcome to Shadow Squadron, Sergeant," Cross said after he wrapped up the brief career and training history.

"Hoo-rah," the men said in unison, echoing the sentiment.

Lancaster nodded, looking far more relaxed than she had when she'd first entered. She took her seat, and Cross began to lay out the extensive cohesion training to come.

* * *

Shepherd, Walker, and Cross were the last to leave the briefing room when the meeting was over. The soldiers had the next couple of hours to themselves, and Lancaster had been dismissed down to Supply to get her new equipment and speak to the tailor about her Shadow Squadron uniform.

The standard Air Force uniform she'd worn in the field had been cut for a male body and didn't fit her quite right. One of the benefits of being part of Shadow Squadron was having a distinct field uniform that was also specifically tailored to each individual.

Shepherd was lingering by the door. "Say, Commander, Chief?" he said to Walker and Cross. "Can I ask you something about Morgan?"

"Speak your mind, Sergeant," Cross said.

"Did you know we knew each other?" Shepherd said. "Me and Morgan, I mean."

"I didn't know about you and her sister," Cross answered. "I saw you went to the same high school at the same time, though. As small as your graduating class was, it seemed likely you'd met at least."

"That doesn't have anything to do with why you picked her, does it?" Shepherd asked. "Did you think that maybe since I knew her that'd make it easier for the other guys to accept her as a teammate?"

"The thought crossed my mind," Cross admitted.

"Well, do me a favor, Commander," Shepherd said. "Don't tell her that."

"Don't worry, Sergeant," Cross said. "This team doesn't need a kid sister or a mascot. It needs a good soldier who can do the work. Lancaster's proven to me that she's legit, and I'm fully confident she can prove the same to you and the others on her own. Without your help."

Shepherd nodded. "Good. I'm glad to hear you say that, Sir," he said. "Lord knows I already have enough sisters of my own to worry about back home."

Walker frowned. "I'm willing to bet your sisters worry about you even more," he said.

Shepherd nodded. "Fair enough."

* * *

Two weeks into Shadow Squadron's cohesion training, Cross called an unexpected meeting in the briefing room. He saw confusion on every face as the team filed in — even Chief Walker's. Cross hoped they couldn't read the aggravation and frustration in his face.

"Change of plans," he said when everyone was seated. Fortunately, he didn't add "gentlemen" this time, which he'd been doing for most of the past two weeks whenever he addressed the group. *Little victories,* he thought. "We've got a priority mission that puts cohesion training on hold for now. Word just came through this morning. From high up."

"How high?" Chief Walker asked. "Command tends to give us our space during training."

"True," Cross said. He took a deep breath to stifle a frustrated sigh. "But Command's hands are tied on this one. By the purse strings."

"Oh," Walker said, reading between the lines. Yamashita nodded knowingly as well, but the others looked confused.

"I've been on the phone half the night with Senator Jason Barron," Cross explained. "For those of you who don't know, he's the head of the sub-committee that controls our little program's secret budget." With that, all remaining confusion vanished from around the table.

"Yesterday afternoon," Cross said, "Senator Barron received this voicemail." Cross tapped the touchpad on the table. Instantly, a scratchy and static-garbled voice came from the room's speakers.

"Dad, it's Jack…Temedt office in Tessalit…have to help… I told them about my trust fund…by wire in one week…bad connection…sorry."

"That's it?" Walker asked after the recording ended.

"It's all the Senator's techs could make out," Cross said.

"It's authentic?" Walked asked.

"Senator Barron is sure it's his son's voice, but the original recording is even worse than this one. It tracks, though. His son's been in Mali — which is where the city of Tessalit is — since he graduated college. He's been working with the Temedt group in an effort to raise awareness of slavery over there."

"So Barron's worried something's happened to his son?" Staff Sergeant Adam Paxton asked.

Walker nodded. "He probably doesn't like the sound of 'have to help,'" he said.

"That's exactly it," Cross said. "The Senator doesn't know any details, but he believes his son is in some sort of danger. Specifically, he's convinced himself that Jack's been kidnapped. Likely by some group of slavers the local Temedt office has gone up against. Jack has a trust fund set up by his grandfather, and Senator Barron believes the fact that his son mentioned it indicates there's a ransom demand involved here."

"But he isn't certain," Yamashita said flatly.

"Right," Cross said. "Neither the son nor any alleged kidnappers have been back in contact with him since. So they came to us."

"So what's the Senator want from us?" Shepherd asked.

"He wants our boots on the ground," Cross said. "We're to get into Mali, find his son, and bring him back home."

"Assuming he's been kidnapped," Paxton said.

"Assuming he's even still alive," Yamashita added.

"Right," Cross said again, his voice grim. "Should that not be the case, we're to 'find, root out, and punish the evildoers.' The Senator's words, not mine."

"Why us?" Paxton asked.

"Fair question," Cross said. "As the Senator explains it, no other team has the proper motivation to see this done as well and quickly as we do."

Cross saw his expression of distaste mirrored in the faces around the table.

Yamashita broke the silence. "Meaning that Senator Barron is prepared to hold our budget hostage so we'll do what he wants," he said. "Ironic."

"Yeah," Cross said. "Very ironic."

"To think I voted for that guy," Lancaster muttered.

Walker looked up at Lancaster. For a moment, Cross expected him to growl a warning at Lancaster the way he always had whenever Brighton had made smart remarks. Instead, the Chief burst out laughing. The others joined in as well, trading surprised looks around the table. Even Yamashita chuckled, which was a rarity all on its own. Lancaster scratched the back of her neck self-consciously and looked up at Cross with an apologetic shrug.

"All right, all right," Cross said. "Settle down. We have a trip and a blind operation to plan. And if the Senator's deductions are accurate, we've got less than a week to pull this thing off."

Cross activated the table's touchpad once again. A world map appeared on the whiteboard. Cross touched a light stylus to Mali up in the northwest of Africa. Another tap broke the Mali map into its eight administrative regions, and Cross selected one of the two regions in the eastern portion.

"This is the Kidal Region," he said, centering it on the display. "In 2011, Tuareg and Islamist rebels tried to turn the entire northern half of Mali, including Kidal, into an independent region called Azawad. The Malian government was losing ground there, but then began taking it back by degrees with the French military's aid. Meanwhile, the Tuaregs have been fighting the Islamists as the Islamists have been trying to lay down sharia law in the region. US forces have been on the sidelines monitoring the Islamists for any connections that might arise to Al-Qaeda or other terrorist groups."

Lancaster nodded at that last part. She'd most recently been stationed across the eastern border in Niger as part of that effort, as well as to lend occasional aid to French forces active in Mali.

"Long story short," Cross continued, "it's a mess over there. The local armies on both sides of the conflict are a shambles, and law enforcement is iffy at best. And the farther north you go, the deeper you get into the desert, which means communities are smaller and farther apart. Very Wild West. Slavery is an issue as well. It's against local law, but it also has a strong historical and traditional backbone. Organizations like this Temedt group that the Senator's son mentioned are doing what they can to combat it, but the farther you get from solid government control, the harder it is to wipe out.

Cross touched his stylus to the whiteboard. "This is Tessalit, the rural commune at the center of the district. Most of the greater area is either desert plains or part of the Adrar des Ifoghas mountain range; the commune is at an oasis in the mountains. This is Jack Barron's last known location. According to his own social media updates, he moved out there from Timbuktu last June. Our intelligence suggests that the mountain badlands of Adrar des Ifoghas are home to scattered camps of rebels fleeing Malian and French forces."

Cross took a breath and paused before continuing the

briefing. The next part would be a tricky aspect of the mission. "If there are slaver groups operating in the area, they could be hiding there just as well," he said. "We'll start our investigation here and borrow some recon time from satellite flyovers and the drones we have on station in Niger to help us keep an eye over the mountains. Command's already arranging for the satellite time. Lancaster, you'll be on point arranging the drone surveillance."

"Sir," Lancaster said.

"There's not much else to say at this point that we can't go over in flight," Cross said. "This is a blind operation with a tight deadline. We'll have more information on local contacts and a full aerial recon picture by the time we arrive. After that, all we can do is wait and see and react. So get your gear. We've got an hour before our first flight takes off."

* * *

In no time at all, the team gathered its gear and boarded two of its state-of-the-art CV-22B Ospreys for the long trip to Mali. The Osprey could take off and land like a standard airplane or vertically like a helicopter. With its extended range and additional wing fuel tanks, the Osprey was able to cross the Atlantic and make it all the way to Africa in one uninterrupted flight, slowing only for in-flight refueling.

That's not to say the ride was a particularly comfortable one. The flight crew, half of Shadow Squadron, and half the team's gear filled much of each Osprey. In addition, each cargo compartment carried an M1161 Growler. The vehicle was a light utility, light strike, fast-attack model much like a Jeep, but slimmer and with less armor.

Shadow Squadron actually touched ground first in Niger after a fast flyover of Mali. The trip added their planes' own forward-looking infrared radar imagery to the growing cache of aerial reconnaissance Cross and Lancaster had arranged for. The Ospreys set down at the small airfield that Lancaster had helped set up when she'd been assigned there by the Air Force. A handful of technicians crawled over the aircraft like ants to check for signs of wear and tear after the long flight.

By the time the checkup was finished, the Ospreys had been subtly transformed from long-haul workhorses to sleek, short-range birds of prey. The team then climbed back in to head west into Mali.

"You didn't want to catch up with your old pals?" Shepherd asked Lancaster once their Osprey was airborne again. Lancaster had spent most of the brief layover fiddling with the special gear she'd packed for the trip. "You were stationed here, right?"

"That was almost two years ago," Lancaster said. "All the guys I worked with have rotated out to other assignments. Besides, what could I even tell them about my new job?"

Cross overheard that and nodded grimly to himself. It was a hard fact of military life that the more elite and specialized a soldier became, the harder it became to relate to those soldiers outside one's immediate team or others at the same level of specialization. And it didn't get more specialized than the

black-level secrecy under which Shadow Squadron operated. Lancaster didn't seem especially troubled by what she said, merely a little wistful, but Cross made a mental note to bring up the topic after cohesion training.

In no time at all, the Ospreys arrived in Tessalit. A few team members fast-roped down to secure the landing zone. A moment later, the Ospreys touched down on a raggedy airstrip on the fringe of the Tessalit commune.

When the Growlers were unloaded and Shadow Squadron had divided its personnel and gear into them, Cross gave the Osprey pilots their orders and led the expedition into Tessalit. The first stop would be the local Temedt office. Cross hadn't been able to make contact with the office by phone while en route. He hoped an in-person visit would prove more fruitful.

The office, when they finally found it, was nothing to write home about. It was a plain, brown, and square stone building that looked just like the ones to either side and across the street. Inside, a teenage girl doggedly pedaled a stationary bike connected by belts to the ceiling fans that did nothing to cool the air but at least kept it circulating. She spoke neither English nor French, but Walker spoke in Bambara and learned that the head of operations was in his office in the back.

The head of operations made no secret that he was not pleased to see soldiers in his office, but he told Cross what he wanted to know. Jack Barron and his partner, a local man named Pierre Sanogo, were on a charity outreach mission in a distant village named Cadran Solaire. The Temedt officer was surprised that Barron might have been kidnapped, claiming he'd heard nothing of the sort. Barron hadn't checked in yet this week, but he wasn't expected back in Tessalit before Saturday. The Temedt officer offered to arrange a place for Cross and his soldiers to stay if they wanted to wait until then, but Cross declined. All Cross wanted was a location, directions, and local maps to compare against his own. When he got those, the team set out again.

An hour later, the Growlers pulled into Cadran Solaire. It was a modest collection of small, square, one-story stone buildings nestled into the crook of a sandstone valley with a single narrow pass on the far side. In one corner of the valley lay a deep, still pond of fresh water. A crooked spear of wind-smoothed stone rose out from the water as tall as a pine tree. Twelve round, flat rocks had been placed around the edge of the pond in a circle, each carved with Roman numerals representing the hours of the day. It was easily the biggest sundial Cross had ever seen.

A group of maybe a dozen children played soccer in the dusty street. As Shadow Squadron pulled in, the kids stopped to stare, blocking the Growlers' path. They crowded around the vehicles, chattering excitedly in Bambara, speaking to the soldiers as if they expected them to understand their language. Cross had no idea what they were saying, but he did catch a few words: *Légion étrangère* in French. He cut his Growler's engine and signaled for Chief Walker to do the same. They stepped out, leaving their vehicles where they stood.

"We're looking for Jack Barron," Cross told the assembled crowd in heavily accented French. "Or maybe Pierre Sanogo. They're from Temedt."

Walker repeated the question in Bambara. As the name penetrated the crowd, a chill seemed to settle on the kids. They became strangely reserved and took hold of the soldiers' hands to pull them toward the village.

The procession filed into the village past a few wary-looking adults standing in front of their homes in the shade of makeshift awnings. A man in a loose, sleeveless robe met them halfway. He greeted them politely enough but asked them bluntly why they'd come. When Walker told the man who they were looking for, the man backed off without a word and let the children continue leading the way.

When the kids finally gave way, they were at a building near the narrow canyon that led out the far side of the village. A Jeep larger and heavier than Shadow Squadron's Growlers sat parked outside it. The Jeep had a heavy machine gun mounted on the back. Two men in Malian army uniforms without rank or company insignia lounged against the Jeep, chatting in low tones. When Cross and then Walker tried to ask who the men were, the children either pretended ignorance or acted like they didn't see anyone. They were adamant that Barron and Sanogo were inside the building, however, so Cross and Walker thanked them and sent them back off to play. The kids merely retreated to a safe distance to see what would happen next.

"Chief, with me," Cross said, nodding toward the building. "Everybody else, keep an eye out."

With Walker behind him, Cross went in to find Jack Barron. The building was someone's home, he found. A low table, washbasin, and clay oven dominated the main area. A sleeping area lay sectioned off behind a ratty cotton curtain. Seated at the table in the main room was a hard, muscular man in plain fatigues like those on the men by the Jeep. A FAMAS bullpup rifle stood leaning against the table in arm's reach. Across from him sat a local man in civilian clothes and a foreigner who could only be Jack Barron.

Barron looked quite different from the clean-shaven college kid in his father's reference photos. Gone were the polo shirt and chinos and the sixty-dollar haircut. Now he wore a faded cloth shirt over khaki cargo pants. His sun-bleached hair hung down past his ears in limp, disordered curls. His skin had been baked earthenware brown everywhere except around his eyes and in two bars over his ears. The skin there was still mushroom-stalk white from his overprotective eyewear. His arms were skinny like a monkey's and his long-fingered hands couldn't seem to stay at rest, even in the moment of surprise when Cross and Walker entered.

"Jack Barron?" Cross said, pointedly ignoring the other men. "US military. Got a minute?"

"Aww, man," Barron groaned. "My dad sent you, right?

* * *

"Clearly I haven't been kidnapped," Barron said, as if he were explaining things to a child. "Didn't my father tell you?"

Cross, Walker, and Barron had stepped out of the house and were huddled off to one side speaking in low tones. Barron's partner, Pierre Sanogo, and the man in fatigues remained inside to continue their business. Jannati and Yamashita waited by the

door of the house while the rest of Shadow Squadron milled about waiting for orders. Shepherd seemed to be locked in a staring contest with one of the men guarding the armed Jeep.

"Your father wasn't very clear on your condition," Cross said through his teeth. "He neglected to tell us he spoke to you after that voicemail you sent him."

"Weird," Barron said. "Why would he do that?"

"I'd love to know," Cross said. "What did you talk about?"

"Work," Barron said, maybe too quickly. "And my trust fund. Mostly that."

"What about it?" Walker asked.

"I was trying to get Dad to give me some money out of it," Barron said. "My grandfather's will makes him the trustee, but I'm supposed to be able to decide how the money gets spent. Until I turn 25, though, I can't get any money without my dad's approval."

"What did you want it for?" Walker asked.

"Work," Barron said quickly, breaking eye contact. "You know, work-related stuff."

"You want to donate it to Temedt," Cross said.

"Yeah," Barron said. "You know, for the cause and all that."

"But he wouldn't okay it?" Cross asked. Barron shook his head. Cross added, "And what happened when he told you that? I imagine you argued."

"More than that," Barron said. "I told him I was going to call my lawyer. If my cell phone hadn't died, I would have done it right then. As it is, I'll have to wait 'til Saturday when Pierre and I are back in Tessalit."

"You're not going to have to wait," Cross said. "We've got a sat-phone. Once I get off line with Command, you, me, and your father are going to have a little talk. Chief, keep an eye on him."

Cross stalked away to make the call to Command, leaving Walker and Barron alone. While he waited for the computer to recognize his voice and access code, he listened to Walker and Barron talk.

"I don't get it," Barron said. "Is your captain ticked at me?"

"He's not a captain," Walker said. "And it's not you. If there's anybody who's going to get an earful, it's your father. He pulled some pretty important strings to send us racing over here to rescue you from trouble he knew you weren't actually in. Senator or no, your father has a lot to answer for."

You got that right, Cross thought. He kept his voice relatively calm and professional when he got his Command contact on the line, but he insisted that Command conference in the Senator without delay.

Before Cross could get the Senator on the line, a commotion demanded his attention and he had to hang up. Shouts in English, French, and Bambara had erupted from the house where they'd found Barron. One of the voices belonged to Jannati, whom Cross had sent to keep an eye on things by the door. When Cross looked over, neither Yamashita nor Jannati were where he'd left them, and the other members of his team were stirring themselves to confused action by the door.

Cross had taken no more than a step in that direction when the man who'd been meeting with Barron and Sanogo staggered backward out the door and fell on his backside in the dusty street. Jannati emerged a second later and kicked the man in the back as he tried to roll away. Yamashita and Pierre Sanogo came out next. Sanogo looked horrified and reached out to pull Jannati back from the man on the ground, but Yamashita stopped Sanogo with a firm hand in the center of his chest. The sniper's eyes scanned from Jannati to the man on the ground and then over to the Jeep the man had arrived in. He cocked an eyebrow at Shepherd.

Cross then saw what the sniper had seen. The two men who'd been guarding the Jeep were scrambling into action, hurriedly yanking the FAMAS rifles slung over their shoulders and into their hands. Fortunately, Paxton and Shepherd saw the same thing. Stepping apart, they raised their M4 carbines and barked sharp orders for the two men to stand down. Hospital Corpsman Second Class Kyle Williams followed suit when he saw what the two Green Berets were doing. Lancaster hesitated, looking from Jannati to Cross and then back to the two FAMAS-armed men before raising her weapon. The two Jeep guards stopped and pointed their rifles at the dirt, glancing at each other uncertainly.

Jannati pushed the man back to the ground with another kick. The Malian yelped but remained on his knees.

"Lieutenant!" Cross yelled at Jannati. "Stand down!"

Jannati backed away just slightly out of kicking range, but his face was still a mask of rage.

Walker ordered the two Jeep guards in Bambara to drop their weapons. He held his weapon across his chest and stood in front of Jack Barron, shielding him.

Finding themselves outgunned, the Jeep guards lay down their weapons and then backed off. Shepherd looked at Lancaster and nodded toward the weapons. She gathered them up and carried them over to Cross.

Cross stalked toward Jannati and stopped opposite the man Jannati had kicked. "Explain yourself," Cross said firmly.

"Let this one explain it," Jannati said, throwing an accusatory glare at Pierre Sanogo. He gave a second one to Barron. "Or maybe the fortunate son over there."

"I said explain yourself," Cross growled.

Jannati gritted his teeth, but Cross could tell the Marine wasn't angry with him. Jannati took a deep breath to compose himself, but the look of outrage returned when he glanced at the Malian at his feet.

"I overheard this piece of work talking in there while you and the Senator's kid were outside," Jannati began. "He's a slaver thug. He was trying to extort money from Temedt to leave this village alone. He's running a protection racket."

Although he wasn't as worked up as Jannati, Yamashita nodded his confirmation with a cold, faraway look in his eyes.

Cross heard Barron suck in a horrified breath. Sanogo looked similarly stricken, but he only hung his head, the shame in his eyes failing to deny the accusation. Neither man looked surprised by Jannati's revelation but rather dismayed that the secret had come out in front of other people.

"So you just decided to go cowboy justice on him?" Cross demanded. "This isn't why we're here, Lieutenant."

Jannati couldn't have looked more surprised if Cross had slapped him. "Sir, I —"

"Quiet! I don't care what this two-bit lowlife is up to. He's not the mission." Cross pointed at Barron. "*He* is the mission. And frankly, I'm getting to the point where I don't care what happens to him, either."

Barron gulped. Jannati winced. Cross pressed on. "Now take Mister Sanogo back in the house," he said. He made a gesture taking in Jannati and Yamashita. "I want the pair of you to keep an eye on him, but keep your hands to yourself. You read me?"

"Sir," Yamashita said. Jannati said the same, though it took him a few seconds to compose himself enough to say so.

"And you," Cross said in French to the Malian half-crouched in the dirt. "You understand me? Get up."

The Malian did so, glaring at Cross with plain hatred. "I don't care who you are or what you're doing here," Cross told the man. "Get your men, get in your Jeep, and get lost. I don't want to see you again before we fly out of here."

The Malian's eyes narrowed but he nodded. He hobbled over to his comrades, who looked just as helpless and defeated as he did.

"Sergeant," Cross said to Lancaster without taking his eyes off the wounded Malian. "Go make sure there's nothing else in their Jeep that we don't want there."

Lancaster tilted her head at Cross's order, hesitating. A moment later, she nodded and did as told, leaving the two FAMAS rifles on the ground near Cross. When she reached the Jeep, Cross called out to the three Malians in French again.

"Hey, look at me," he called. "We're keeping these guns. I'm sure you've got more back home, but I strongly suggest you don't bring them back here."

The Malians grumbled and frowned, but they knew they were in no position to protest. When Lancaster finished with their vehicle, she backed off to let the Malians climb into it. They peeled out, tearing off through the sandstone canyon in a cloud of dust. Cross looked around to make sure his people were all right. He noticed that all of the locals had scattered into hiding. *Probably for the best,* Cross thought.

"What did you just do?" Barron asked in a scared, small voice. "You have no idea who that is."

"Let me guess," Cross replied, "that's why you actually wanted your trust fund. Protection money."

"Not that it matters now," Barron grumbled.

"You told your father as much?" Cross continued.

"I tried to explain how things work over here," Barron said, "but he just said, 'You don't negotiate with these people, son. It only emboldens them.'"

"He's got a point," Cross said. "The more money you give people like that, the more they're going to want. Eventually they'll bleed you dry if you don't stand up to them."

"That's easy for you to say," Barron said. "You don't live here. Plus, you've got the Army behind you. What do these people have? Not much against that guy you just humiliated in front of all of them. Do you know who he even is? His name's *Bubaga*, but the locals call him the Spider. He's not just some slave broker. He runs guns and does protection rackets and human trafficking over three regions. He's got an entire army he formed from rebel deserters and mercenaries the government couldn't afford to pay anymore. Bubaga is a dangerous man, but for all that, he's at least honorable. He respects money, and I've got more than plenty to spare. I could've handled this if you hadn't interfered."

"Except you don't have that money," Cross said. "Your father wouldn't sign off on it, right? If you told him what you're doing here and who you're dealing with, that's probably why he sent us out here. He didn't want you to have to deal with Bubaga when you couldn't deliver the money you promised."

"I could've explained things," Barron said weakly.

"Unlikely," Walker said, returning. He looked at Cross and said, "Ospreys are on the way, Sir."

"What's an Osprey?" Barron asked.

"It's our ride out of here," Cross said. "And yours too, if you want it."

"Wait, what?" Barron said. "You're just…leaving?"

"Yep," Cross said. "Full of sound and fury. As far as I'm concerned, this mission's over. You're accounted for and free, so my team's done here. You're welcome to fly out with us, of course, but you're not obligated. You're a grown man."

"Bubaga is coming back here, you know," Barron said. "You understand that, right? He's going to wait until he sees you leave, then he's going to come back with his men to punish these people for what you did. Don't you think you have a responsibility to deal with that? Especially since one of yours caused the problem in the first place?"

"What I think is that I'm getting my people in the air when our ride gets here," Cross said. "You can go with us or you can stay here. The choice is yours."

"Fine then!" Barron spat. "Go! But I'm not abandoning these people. You can go home if you want, but good luck explaining to my father what you're letting happen."

Cross turned away without a word, signaling to Walker. The two of them walked away to gather up the men, collect the Growlers, and wait for the Ospreys to take them away from Cadran Solaire.

The team's Ospreys traversed the darkening Malian sky. "Speak your mind, Lieutenant," Cross said to Jannati. He hadn't said a word since the Ospreys had arrived in Cadran

Solaire. Also on his Osprey were Lancaster and Yamashita. The other Osprey carried Walker, Shepherd, Paxton and Williams. Lancaster sat hunched over her laptop computer, the glow from the screen illuminating her face.

"We can't just leave them there, Commander," Jannati said. He was no longer scowling or frowning, but he still didn't look happy. "Those people have no idea what this guy is going to do to them."

"I agree completely, Lieutenant," Cross said. He'd spent the first several minutes of the flight getting back in touch with Command to request any available intelligence on this Bubaga character. The file Command had sent back read like something out of a comic book villain's biography. Bubaga's wartime atrocities were almost as bad as the crimes Bubaga's own gang had wrought against the civilians who defied him.

"That's why we're not leaving," Cross said.

Jannati blinked. "I beg your pardon, Sir?"

"If we were just turning tail and going home, we could've driven the Growlers back to the air field," Cross explained. "Bringing the Ospreys in and dusting off like we did was all for show. I wanted Bubaga to see us leaving and think the village is undefended."

"You're sure he was watching?" Jannati asked.

"Lancaster?" Cross said.

"His Jeep stopped about half a mile outside Cadran Solaire and waited there until we'd lifted off and were out of sight,"

Lancaster said, looking up from her laptop. "He took up his original heading after that. I'll let you know when he stops again."

Jannati looked at Lancaster, clearly confused. "I put a tracker on his car when I was pretending to search it for weapons," Lancaster told Jannati. "Well, I searched it too. But I also placed the tracker."

Cross was pleased Lancaster had read his implied instructions without needing them spelled out.

"So we're going back to the village?" Jannati asked.

"No," Cross said. "We're going to assume this guy's coming back there as soon as he gets to his hideout, rearms, and gathers his men. We're going to set down in his path and intercept him. If we do this right, the villagers shouldn't be aware of what's going on until it's already over."

Cross activated the high-definition teleconference screen mounted on the wall. On it appeared a cargo-bay view of the other Osprey as seen from the perspective of its own teleconference screen. Walker was visible on-screen, and the other three soldiers with him were gathered around him.

"We're ready here, Sir," the Chief said. "Do we know where the target's headed yet?"

Cross looked at Lancaster. She swiped something from her laptop's touch-sensitive screen toward the Osprey's teleconference screen. A digital contour map of local terrain appeared on half of the screen. A blinking dot labeled with a radio frequency ID appeared, moving through a narrow path through the mountain. The dot represented the tracker Lancaster had hidden on Bubaga's car.

"The path he's on dead-ends into that mountain," Lancaster said. "I don't see any signs of a base, though. My best guess from available aerial recon is that it leads into a cave system or just a complex where he's settled his slaving network."

"Or a *web*," Walker said. "You know, because he's called the Spider." Cross stared blankly at Walker. "Sorry, Commander. Go ahead."

Cross finally allowed himself to grin. *The Chief must miss Brighton,* Cross thought. *Now he's the one cracking bad jokes.*

"Anyway," Cross said. "I'm not keen to chase this guy and his mercenary thugs down into unfamiliar caves in the dead of night. Instead, we'll meet him halfway when he sets out for Cadran Solaire."

Cross dragged his fingertips along the half of the teleconference screen showing the digital aerial map, moving the image backward along the path Bubaga's Jeep had taken.

"Here," he said. The part of the road he'd indicated cut a blind curve through a sandstone pass with a steep wall on the inner curve. There was a sharp, shorter embankment on the outer side. "Chief, you got it?"

Walker tapped his screen, making a blip appear on Cross's screen. "Got it."

"This is where we'll hit them. We'll park one of the

Growlers here." Cross tapped the screen, leaving a bright dot on the map. "This'll be Attack One. If we can blow part of this rock wall down to block the road when they get there, that would be ideal. Lancaster, you and the Chief will assess the terrain."

"Sir," Walker and Lancaster replied.

"I want the other Growler here. This is Attack Two." He tapped the screen again. "Right around this blind curve where they won't see it until it's too late. I'm going to need a volunteer to man that gun."

"Yo," Shepherd said, raising his hand.

"It's yours, Sergeant," Cross told him with a grateful nod. Shepherd hadn't chosen the easy job. If Attack Two had to pull double-duty as a roadblock, it was going to be terribly exposed. Cross turned to Yamashita and indicated another area on the map that was near the ambush site. "Lieutenant, I was thinking here for overwatch. Is this close enough?"

"What's the scale on this map?" Yamashita asked.

"Oops, sorry," Lancaster said. She tapped a few keys on her laptop, and a scale measurement appeared in the bottom corner of the screen.

Yamashita peered at the screen. "It'll do."

"Good. Lancaster, once you set the explosives, take Four-Eyes and go with Yamashita. You'll keep in constant contact with the Ospreys in case we need their firepower for support. I don't want you down in the soup on this one, though."

"Sir?" Lancaster asked, looking insulted.

"I'm not being chivalrous, Sergeant," Cross told her. "You haven't finished cohesion training with us yet. Until you do, you're on overwatch."

"Oh," Lancaster said with a quick nod. "Sir."

"Paxton, set up here at Cover One," Cross went on, indicating another section of the map just behind the ambush point. "If they try to run and get past us, you're the goalie."

"Sir," Paxton said.

"Williams, Cover Two's going to be here," Cross said. "Our gunners are going to be the most exposed when the shooting starts, so I want you to be where you can get to them fast. You've also got a partially covered route out to Cover One if Paxton gets hit."

Williams nodded. "Sir," the medic added.

"Jannati, you'll be on the gun at Attack One."

"Hoo-rah," Jannati said, his eyes dancing.

"Chief, you and I will drive the Growlers into position and support the gunners."

"Sounds good," Walker said.

Without another word, Cross turned to go and give orders to the Ospreys' flight crews.

* * *

The sun had set when Bubaga's men left their base for their intended retaliation against Cadran Solaire. The new moon sky glowed with a dusting of countless stars, and the sound of engines carried for miles through the darkness.

"They're coming, Commander," Lancaster said through her canalphone. From her vantage at overwatch, Lancaster was watching the road through the camera of the remote-controlled "Four-Eyes" quad-copter.

Cross lay in the dirt at Attack One a few yards away from the Growler manned by Aram Jannati. Cross's M4 carbine was propped on his half-empty backpack. His AN/PSQ-20 nightvision lens painted the ambush point in shades of bright green. "How many are there?" Cross asked.

"Five full Jeeps, one man each on the .50 cals," Lancaster reported. "There's an ACMAT truck behind them. It has a large cage on the back."

"Is it empty?" Cross asked.

"Yessir."

"Noted," Cross said. "Seems Bubaga intends to bring the survivors back to his base as slaves."

"That ACMAT could work to block the road behind the Jeeps," Yamashita said over the channel.

"Make it happen when we drop the roadblock in front," Cross said. "Cover One, move to Cover Two."

"Sir," Paxton replied. A moment later, he reported that he was at his new position.

Another few minutes after that, Lancaster reported that the Jeeps were right around the corner. Cross ordered his soldiers to get ready. The engine noise was right on top of them, and the Jeeps' headlights shone from around the blind corner. Cross lifted his nightvision lens so the headlights wouldn't blind him. "Contact. Roadblock ready."

"Ready, Sir," Lancaster said.

The first Jeep's headlights passed right under the high sandstone shelf where Cross and Jannati's Growler was perched. No one in the Jeep seemed to notice them waiting up there. Nor did they spot Attack Two ahead. Two more Jeeps rounded the corner. Then two more. The ACMAT came last.

"Close the road," Cross said.

"Sir," Lancaster said.

Cross looked away as the C4 plastic explosives exploded ahead of the Jeeps. The night shook with a heavy boom. Rocks the size of barrels tumbled into the road. A cloud of dust billowed out in all directions.

A second later, a muted crack sounded at the rear of the slaver convoy. Cross saw the windshield of the ACMAT shatter inward as Yamashita eliminated the driver with a silenced shot from his M110 sniper rifle. The truck nosed toward the edge of the road and coasted to a stop, blocking the way out. The five Jeeps were now trapped between it and the rockslide.

"Attack One, Attack Two," Cross said. "Go."

Jannati and Shepherd opened up with the Growler's

guns, cutting into the first and last vehicles in the line. Jannati targeted the ACMAT's hood with a laser-accurate stream of 7.62x55mm NATO rounds from the minigun, blowing the engine to smithereens so no one could drive away. From farther up, Shepherd sprayed a second stream into the lead Jeep. The driver of that vehicle slammed on his brakes as Shepherd's bullets tore into the side of the vehicle and sent gouts of black smoke pouring from under its hood.

The Jeeps left in the middle lurched to a stop, and the men within reacted in a semi-coordinated panic. The second one backed up a few feet and made as if to try to maneuver around the smoking hulk of the first Jeep. Its headlights washed directly over Attack Two, illuminating Shepherd at the M134 and Walker in a shooter's crouch behind a rock. The third Jeep backed into the fourth, which was trying to move around to follow the second. The man at the fourth Jeep's machine gun fell off, and the third Jeep's gunner fired a burst in the air as he clung to the weapon for balance. The fifth Jeep remained where it was, and the men inside leaped out to return fire.

"Flares!" Cross called over the din.

"Sir!" Lancaster called over the canalphone.

A second later, a set of magnesium lights lit up the desert night. The flares had been Lancaster's idea. Hidden on the road all along the ambush site and detonated by remote, they blazed to furious life among the startled would-be raiders. At such close quarters, the near light blinded the Malians and made their distant targets nearly impossible to see. From outside the immediate area of effect, the light illuminated the Malians perfectly, making them better targets.

"Fire at will," Cross said quietly.

Thunder shattered the night. Walker shot down the machine gunner on the destroyed lead Jeep. The gunner on the fifth Jeep tried to return fire on Attack One through the magnesium glare. Most of his shots were wide to the left, but Cross heard a few dig into the Growler's rear end. Jannati turned his weapon on him, cutting him down and shredding the vehicle. Those who made it out of the Jeep threw themselves flat, scrambling for cover behind the other vehicles.

Of the two Jeeps that had collided, only one gunner remained in position, and he swiveled his barrel up back toward Attack One. The gunner of the Jeep facing Attack Two opened up, spraying wildly. Some of the bullets tore into Walker's cover, forcing the Chief to dive out of the way. Fire from Shepherd's minigun knocked the shooter from the back of the Jeep.

Cross picked off the gunner between the two collided vehicles. Jannati fired on the rearmost of the two Jeeps to keep the gunner who'd fallen off from trying to reclaim his firing position. The gunner retreated toward what minimal cover he could find. Most of the passengers of the two collided Jeeps made it out unharmed, though a burst from Paxton's M4 from his position at Cover Two caught the last one out before he could close the door.

"Frag out!" Williams called.

Paxton hurled an M67 fragmentation grenade into the space between the rear bumper and grill of the two collided Jeeps. The blast made the vehicles jump apart, throwing a hail of steel fragments into the slavers hiding behind them.

"Suppressing fire," Cross ordered. "Attack Two, move down to flank."

"Sir," Walker replied.

As heavy fire from both miniguns ate away at the Jeeps like starving wolves, Cross and Walker came down to road level from their cover positions at opposite ends of the ambush site. Cross came down behind the disabled ACMAT truck and put it between himself and his men. Walker came down along the inside of the fallen-stone roadblock and took cover behind the first Jeep. The magnesium flares were still burning, but thick smoke from the vehicles and brownish dust from the C4 explosion hung in the air, reducing visibility. Cross lifted his M4 to the ready and began to make his way forward.

"Oh, right, right," Lancaster said in Cross's canalphone, likely in response to Yamashita's silent urging. "Sir, you've got what looks like…seven hostiles still moving down there."

No sooner were the words out of Lancaster's mouth than the passenger door of the half-destroyed Jeep nearest Cross fell off. A Malian lurched out with an assault rifle clutched under one bleeding arm. His weapon was already trained on Cross as he speedily dropped to one knee to take aim.

Yamashita was speedier. The sniper's bullet caught the man in the chest, dropping him at Cross's feet.

"Thanks," Cross said.

"Sir," Yamashita said.

"Make that eight," Lancaster said. "Well, now it's seven."

Cross smirked.

Between the crossfire and the suppressing fire from the team's attack and cover positions, the remaining men of Bubaga's gang didn't stand a chance. Cross understood the grim necessity of the work, but it still sickened him. It was little comfort to think that these men had likely shown no mercy to the people they'd slaughtered or sold into slavery.

As for the so-called Spider, they found him laid out by the roadside near an outcropping of rock, a bullet hole in his chest.

"Looks like he was trying to skitter away," Walker said.

"Damage report," Cross said, allowing the bad joke. He was just glad the unpleasantness was over and done.

"Our Growler's not going anywhere," Jannati said. "The rear end's in a million pieces."

"We'll use the other one to push it onto its Osprey," Cross said. He turned to the team's corpsman. "Kyle?"

"No hits," Williams reported. "One injury. Very minor."

"Injury?" Shepherd said, waving a hand filled with sterile gauze pads. A bright, bloody line had cut his cheek below his left eye. Cross noticed it and cocked an eyebrow, waiting for an explanation. "A chip off the Chief's cover nicked me when they shot it up, Commander."

Cross nodded and turned away. He tapped his canalphone. "Overwatch, report."

"Clear," Yamashita said.

"Clear," Lancaster echoed. "I was about to bring Four-Eyes back here."

"Just land it here and reel in," Cross replied.

"Sir," Lancaster said.

"This was grim, ugly work, team," Cross said to those assembled before him and over the canalphone. "But well done all the same."

Cross felt like he should say something else. Maybe something about the villagers they'd protected by intervening, or something along those lines. But no words seemed to suit the situation. Instead, Cross simply nodded and turned away, switching channels on his canalphone to call the waiting Ospreys. When the call was made, Walker led him aside, looking down the road with a troubled expression.

"What's on your mind, Chief?" Cross asked.

"The base these ones came from," Walker said. "That cave, or whatever it is. Bubaga could have more men down there."

"Maybe," Cross said.

"Or slave prisoners," Walker continued. He pointed at the ruined ACMAT. "The look of this truck makes me think he intended to round up the people of Cadran Solaire and bring them there. If he has a place to hold them..."

"He could already have other people there," Cross finished for him. "It's a possibility, but it's not the mission. Not our mission, anyway."

Walker looked down the road, clearly not pleased.

"Tell you what, Chief," Cross said. "There's a Malian Army base not too far away in Amachach. We'll give them our intel on Bubaga's operation and tell them we got it by working off a tip from Jack Barron. We'll tell them what we did and let them take the credit for it as long as they promise to do two things in return."

"What two things?" Walker asked.

"First, they publicly give credit for the tip to Barron, proclaiming him to be a tireless Temedt crusader saving lives while far from his home. Second, they promise to get down here in force and deal with whatever's left in those caves."

Walker frowned. "Will they go along with that?" he asked.

"I think Command and I can explain the importance of going with the flow on this," Cross said with a smirk.

"I think that would qualify as a happy ending to this mess," the Chief said quietly. He looked up as the sound of distant rotors rose on the wind. "Ospreys are coming. Off to Amachach, then."

"First to Cadran Solaire," Cross corrected. "Barron needs to know the plan. I'm sure he'll be thrilled to know he's about to be a hero."

"His father too," Walker commented dryly. "Think how proud he'll be of his son, the hero."

"I look forward to reading all about it in the news when he breaks the story back home," Cross said.

"If the Senator plays his cards right, that story could win him the next election," Walker said.

Cross sighed. "So much for a happy ending, Chief."

Walker chuckled. "Sorry, Sir."

MISSION DEBRIEFING

OPERATION

SAND SPIDER 5678

MISSION COMPLETE

PRIMARY OBJECTIVE

- Determine location of hostage

- Escort hostage to safety

STATUS

2/3 COMPLETE

SECONDARY OBJECTIVES

x Avoid conflict with local forces

CROSS, RYAN

RANK: Lieutenant Commander
BRANCH: Navy Seal
PSYCH PROFILE: Team leader
of Shadow Squadron. Control
oriented and loyal, Cross insisted
on hand-picking each member of
his squad.

I can't quite say this mission went off as originally planned.
But with all things considered, I'm proud of our performance.
We demonstrated the ability to think on our feet, and each
of you showed you have the composure and adaptability
necessary to be a part of Shadow Squadron. And we made
Cadran Solaire a safer and better place.

Good job, everyone -- especially you, Lancaster. Welcome
to the team.

– Lieutenant Commander Ryan Cross

ERROR
UNAUTHORIZED
USER MUST HAVE LEVEL 12 CLEARANCE
OR HIGHER IN ORDER TO GAIN ACCESS
TO FURTHER MISSION INFORMATION.

2019.681

MISSION BRIEFING

OPERATION

DARK AGENT　　　　　5678

CIA agent Bradley Upton has intel to share with us regarding a particularly dangerous bomb maker nicknamed "the Professor." I've had a few close calls with him in the past, so let's just say I want us to be entirely committed to capturing him once and for all.

We'll head to Yemen immediately and begin setting up a snare to catch this elusive explosives expert.

– Lieutenant Commander Ryan Cross

3245.98

YEMEN

PRIMARY OBJECTIVES

- Locate "the Professor"

- Capture him alive

1932.789

SECONDARY OBJECTIVES

- Maintain covert presence in Yemen

0412.981

1624.054

DARK AGENT

Somewhere in Yemen...

A burst of frigid water splashed into Lieutenant Commander Ryan Cross's face, returning him to consciousness and stealing his breath. He coughed and tried to spit water out his mouth and nose. His confused mind struggled to fight the fear that he was drowning. *Dying.*

The terror passed only after he'd gagged and sneezed out the last bit of water. When he opened his eyes, he saw that he had a new reason to fear for his life. Standing before him was a nightmare from Cross's past. The man held an empty, dripping bucket in his hands.

The man leered at Cross with a twisted mix of delight and hatred. "We've never met," the man said. He spoke in English with an Arabic accent. "And I'd been pleased by that fact. Your reputation precedes you. But now that I have you face-to-face, I don't find you all that fearsome."

Cross had to admit that he didn't feel particularly fearsome at that moment. He had been drugged and beaten. His face was a mask of pain, and his left eye was nearly swollen shut. The canalphone he usually wore nestled in his left ear was gone. He still wore the civilian clothes he'd been wearing when he was taken, but his SIG P226 pistol, his utility knife, and his ballistic vest were all gone. It was the loss of the canalphone that troubled him the most. Without it, he couldn't hear or talk to his team.

Cross's first attempt to speak ended in a retching cough, and he spat up one last spray of water.

"You are lost," Cross's captor said. He was a Middle Eastern man with a scraggly beard and thinning hair. He wore spectacles, and he had dark, beady eyes. The teeth that showed through his sick smile were long and crooked and more yellow than white. Although the face was familiar to Cross, he didn't know the man's real name.

"All the same," the man continued, "a chance at freedom yet remains for you. Perhaps even heroism."

The man stepped back to set aside the bucket. Cross took a look at his surroundings. He was bound to a metal desk chair with plastic zip-ties around both ankles and his left wrist. A nylon rope bound his thighs to the seat. For some reason, his right arm was free.

A glance around revealed that he was in a windowless room. A leather couch was opposite him. A wooden coffee table with a glass top was between them. Bookshelves and standing lamps lined one wall. A brown, red, and yellow carpet lay beneath the coffee table.

The man had moved to the threshold of the open door to Cross's right, which Cross noted was the only way out. "Bring him in," the man said.

Someone outside answered. A moment later, a hunched and hooded figure was shoved into the room. Cross's captor took charge of this second prisoner. The man bound the prisoner's wrists with nylon cord then shut the door behind him. He led the hooded man to the couch and shoved him down. Cross recognized the prisoner's clothing.

"Here lies the gateway to your freedom," their captor said, turning back to Cross. As he spoke, he produced Cross's SIG P226 from beneath his robe and laid it on the coffee table, close to Cross's side. "You need only raise this gun and shoot this man, and you will be free."

"Or I could shoot you," Cross said. "Might be worth it."

"Satisfying to your ego, perhaps," the man said, "but a waste of both our lives. We are not alone here. If your gunshot is not followed immediately by word from me, those who wait outside will come in and kill you both. And you have only one bullet. Enough for him, or for me. But I think you will find killing this one rewarding. For if you kill him, not only will I let you live, but I will turn myself in as well. I will submit myself to American justice, whatever form it takes. The only price is this man's life. Will you pay it?"

"Who is he?" Cross asked, trying to stall.

A malevolent smile twisted the man's face. "I should make

you decide before I answer that," the man said. "I am not so cruel, however."

He lifted the stiff burlap hood from the prisoner's face. The man beneath was just as bruised and bloody as Cross felt. The left lens of his expensive glasses was cracked, and the frame sat crooked on his bleeding nose. He lifted his head, and his eyes met Cross's gaze.

"Ryan," he choked out.

"Agent Upton," Cross said. "Didn't I tell you to stay in the van?"

A weak smile rose to Upton's lips. "I had to pee."

* * *

One Week Earlier...

Cross rubbed his right forearm as he entered the briefing room of Shadow Squadron's headquarters. The room was already full when Cross arrived. He saw Walker hunched over Cross's spot at the head of the conference table. Walker was operating the computer touchpad recessed into the table's surface. At Walker's command, the globe-and-crossed-swords emblem of Joint Special Operations Command bloomed on the computer whiteboard behind him.

Cross normally set up the briefing equipment before a meeting, but last-minute communications with Command and a painful shot in the arm from the base's doctor had delayed him. Fortunately, Walker had taken the initiative in Cross's absence.

A year ago, Walker's initiative might have agitated the Commander. When he'd left the Navy SEALs to join Shadow Squadron, Cross had gotten plenty of static from the Chief. Walker had been second-in-command on his previous team, and he'd expected to take the lead in his next assignment. Instead, the brass at JSOC recruited Cross to fill the leadership spot on Shadow Squadron.

It had been a long, hard road breaking the Chief of the habit of trying to subvert Cross's authority. Harder still had been convincing the older soldier that Cross was the better man for the job. But months of intense training and a long list of successful missions had eventually earned Walker's respect. They'd since forged a bond of brotherhood between them. Cross counted their friendship as one of his greatest accomplishments.

"Morning," Cross said to the group. He began to swipe through icons on the touchpad as Walker ceded the position at the front and took a seat next to Cross.

A blank teleconferencing window popped up on the whiteboard. "New mission for us today," Cross said. "Command says to give it top priority. The CIA's Special Activities Division has identified a high-value Al-Qaeda target operating in Yemen. We're going to go pick him up."

Cross saw questions rising to his soldiers' lips. Rather than answer them all, he tapped the desk touchpad once more to open the teleconference connection. A familiar face appeared. It belonged to a smiling, middle-aged white man with slicked-back hair, a cleft chin, and sporting expensive glasses. The corner of his mouth curled up like he was smirking at the camera. Or directly at Cross.

"Ryan, good morning!" the man said, as if greeting an old friend after a long absence.

"Agent Upton," Cross replied with a nod. He glanced up at his team to gauge their reactions.

Agent Bradley Upton was a longtime Central Intelligence Agency field operative who worked in secret around the world, fighting the war on terror. Working hand-in-glove with the JSOC, Upton helped find the secret places where terrorists armed themselves and executed their plans. His mission was to foil their plans and bring them to justice. His primary center of operations had been Iraq for many years, but since US forces had largely left that country, Upton had transitioned to Yemen.

The CIA operative did most of his work alone, but he coordinated the efforts of several other divisions. Like Shadow Squadron, those teams performed high-risk black ops. The day Cross had been offered leadership of Shadow Squadron, Upton tried to steal him for his own team. Upton had offered greater glory, more operational freedom, and much more money than the Shadow Squadron position offered. Fortunately, Cross had previously worked with Upton and knew what kind of man he really was. That was to say, not a good one.

The rest of Shadow Squadron had gotten to know Upton during their last mission in Iraq. Through favor-trading above Cross's rank, Upton "borrowed" Cross's team for use as bodyguards for an Iraqi CIA informant. The informant had turned out to be a former terrorist who sold information about his former allies in exchange for money, prestige, and political power. He'd also proven himself a coward who'd tried to use his ten-year-old grandson as a sniper shield when assassins had come for him. The fact that Agent Upton had placed such value on the informant's life earned the team's scorn. Cross understood their hostility toward Upton.

Only one person in the room didn't know Upton as anything other than a name on old files. "And this must be Miss Lancaster," the agent said.

"It's Staff Sergeant Lancaster," Walker said with a scowl.

Lancaster looked to the whiteboard and gave a cool nod. Lancaster was one of the first women to enter and graduate from the Air Force Combat Control School. If she took the same offense to Upton's comment that Walker had, she showed no sign of it.

"Staff Sergeant Lancaster," Upton said through an overly sweet smile. "I've read a lot of good things about you. Welcome to the team."

"We're just starting the briefing, Agent Upton," Cross said. "The intel on our target all comes from you. Would you like to do the honors?"

"After you," Upton said. "I'll correct you if you get anything wrong." He smiled again. "Not that I expect you to. You've been very well informed."

Cross didn't like the look of Upton's eyes. They seemed

distant and calculating. No matter how much he smiled and complimented others, no hint of warmth flickered in those cold eyes.

Cross tapped the touchpad once more. A second window appeared beside Upton's, showing a satellite map of the Arabian Peninsula. Cross highlighted Yemen, the country on the peninsula's southwestern corner. As the image appeared on the whiteboard, Cross glanced up at Jannati at the far end of the table. According to Jannati's file, his grandfather had immigrated to America from Yemen in the early 1960s. Surprisingly, the location of the mission hadn't seemed to affect the young soldier.

In a third window, Cross produced a cropped photo showing a man wearing a long gray robe, a crocheted taqiyah cap, and pince-nez spectacles. The man had a scraggly beard and very little hair under his cap. In the photo, he was smiling at something off camera.

"This is our target," the Commander said. "We've never learned his real name or country of origin, but his known associates all call him Ustadh. Word has it he's one of Al-Qaeda's most talented and dangerous bomb makers. He spent most of the war years moving around Iraq teaching the insurgents how to build and plant IEDs, car bombs, and explosive belts. Hence the name."

"Ustadh means 'the professor' in Arabic," Upton added.

"He's slippery, this one," Cross added, "and one I've got some personal experience with. My old SEAL team actually

went after him a few times, but he was always one step ahead of us. Last we heard, he'd died in Baqubah with Abu Musab Al-Zarqawi in 2006."

"That was my mistake, as Ryan seems too polite to say," Agent Upton said. "My people provided an inaccurate report."

"Apparently," Cross said, "one of Zarqawi's lieutenants was misidentified as Ustadh. As soon as we thought he was dead, the Professor fled the country with no one looking for him. Now that he's popped up in Yemen, evidence suggests he's looking to hook up with AQAP."

The terrorist organization known as Al-Qaeda in the Arabian Peninsula (or AQAP) had grown out of the original Al-Qaeda Islamist militant group founded by the late Osama bin Laden. It had perpetrated a long list of bombings and other attacks against Yemeni, Saudi, and American targets. Intel suggested they planned to do far worse in the coming months.

"How solid is this lead?" Walker asked, not bothering to conceal the skepticism in his voice. He'd been frowning since the briefing started — and with good reason. Normally Cross discussed mission plans with him before the two of them brought the specifics to the rest of the team. However, Cross hadn't been able to do so this time around because the arrangement with Upton had been last-minute.

Additionally, Command asked Cross to keep certain information to himself on this mission. Walker didn't like surprises or secrets, especially when they came from higher up the chain of command.

"I wouldn't say I trust the source," Cross said, "but I believe his information is legit."

From his teleconference window on the whiteboard, Upton laughed. No one else joined in.

"I have a question," Paxton said from near the back of the room. Paxton was looking at Cross, but it was Upton who answered. "Ask away, Adam."

Paxton waited for Cross to nod his permission then looked directly into the tiny camera's eye. "Why are you coming to us with this?" Paxton asked. "We've got special forces all over Yemen and the rest of the Middle East these days."

"You've got people of your own too," Shepherd added. "You had half a platoon with you during our mission together in Nasiriyah."

"That was Nasiriyah," Upton said. "I've only been in Yemen a little while. All the same, when we stumbled over Ustadh here, my first thoughts were of your commander. I know how important capturing the Professor is to him. I owe him a chance to be the one to bring him in. It was one of my junior agents who misidentified Ustadh as K.I.A. with Zarqawi in 2006. Thus, letting him get away was my responsibility, and now I've got a chance to make that right. Even if that were all there is to it, that would still be plenty enough for me."

"This bomb maker has escaped from me three different times," Cross said, addressing his soldiers. "The first time, he made me look like the green idiot I was. The second time, he laid a trap in what we thought was his safe house. Three Navy

SEALs died that day. And this last escape was the worst because it was caused by plain human error. He's been laughing behind my back for almost a decade, and I'm sick of it. Agent Upton's got the goods on this guy, so we're going to bring him down once and for all. Ustadh isn't getting away from me again."

Cross paused and took a deep breath. It wasn't like him to make a mission personal, and his team knew that. *Time to dial it back a little,* he thought.

Fortunately, Jannati spoke up first. "We'll get it done, sir."

"Hoo-rah," the rest of the team echoed.

"Ha!" Upton crowed. "Hoo-rah…" He said the word like it tasted sweet. "That's what I like to hear. And to that end, we believe we know where Ustadh is going to be most vulnerable."

"Where?" Cross asked. For all his big promises, Upton had been stingy with concrete details.

"Well, before I answer that," Upton said, feigning embarrassment, "I need to tell you about a recent development on my end. It's not something I'd normally mention, but it does seem to upset you when I don't tell you every little thing right up front."

"What's happened?" Cross said.

Upton shrugged. "There's a slim possibility that the Professor spotted one of my local guys tailing him yesterday morning. There's no indication yet that he knows who we are, but he knows somebody's watching him now. Worse, he disappeared for half the day after that, and we didn't reacquire him until just about an hour after dinner last night. He's back under surveillance, but all the same…"

"At least you didn't lose him," Walker grumbled.

"Again," Upton corrected. "At least I didn't lose him *again*, you mean. But yes, while we didn't have eyes on him, he could have been making arrangements to disappear on us. Frankly, for all we know, he could have been building a suitcase nuke. We don't know what he was doing, and I don't like that. I'd like to accelerate the timetable and make a move on the target sooner rather than later. I'm sure Ryan agrees."

"I do," Cross said.

"And what do you get out of this, Agent Upton?" Yamashita asked. His voice was steady and his face was a neutral mask. Cross, however, knew his sniper well enough to read his eyes. He was burning with contempt for Upton's methods and the company he kept in the name of doing business.

Upton winked. "It's not nothing," he admitted. "Nothing in this life is free."

Cross knew that Upton would expect something in exchange for the opportunity he offered. The fact that Upton hadn't wanted to discuss it until Cross was on the spot in front of his men implied it would be something big.

"The Professor is having a meeting with a suspected AQAP financier Wednesday afternoon at 1:00 PM local time at a historical site in Aden called the Tawila Cisterns. He's cagey on the phone and in his emails, but we think he has been trying to lure the Professor out of retirement for something big that AQAP has planned. Ustadh has been reluctant to draw attention to himself since his reported death, but he's agreed to the meeting anyway."

Cross braced himself. "What do you want?" he ordered.

"What I want," Upton said, "is to have a talk with that financier. I think there's plenty about Al-Qaeda he can tell us. So, your job is going to be to capture him alive and hand him over to me. You do that, and the Professor is all yours."

That price isn't as high as I expected, Cross thought. "We might be able to do that," he said. "I wonder, though, what's keeping JSOC from just sending a team that's already in country to get Ustadh right now, seeing as to how you've already got him under surveillance."

"What's keeping JSOC — and you — from doing so is that you don't know where he's under surveillance. My people are the only ones who do, and I decide who I share that information with," Upton said. "All the same, trust me when I say that Ustadh is too well guarded to just grab. Not that your men aren't talented, Ryan, but he'd know you were coming a mile away."

"Plus, even if we did just grab him," Walker said, "this financier you want so badly would vanish as soon as we did."

"You get a gold star, Chief Walker," Upton said. "That's exactly why you can't have Ustadh until I get my financier. Oh, and just so we're clear, information is our mission priority here. If something should happen to my target or if he should get away, I'll be more than happy to settle for your Professor instead and see what he can tell me under interrogation."

"You're assuming they won't die while resisting capture," Cross said.

"Oh, I have every confidence you won't let that happen," Upton said. "I hate to think how the relationship between our two organizations might be damaged if that ended up being the case. Especially after I brought you into this operation as a personal favor."

"You'll have nothing to worry about," Cross assured him, though he hated the taste of every word he'd spoken. "As for the operation itself, we'll need to unify command of our two teams in the field. How many SOG guys do you have at your disposal these days?"

"Well, about that," Upton said, feigning embarrassment. "I'm a little short-handed just now. Special Activities hasn't put a full SOG team at my disposal here like the one I had in Iraq. I've got an analyst and a junior agent or two I can call, but when it comes to the physical side, I'm short."

"So that's why you called on us," Walker said, not sounding at all surprised.

"In my defense," Upton said, "yours was the first team I thought of."

Cross sighed. Upton hadn't changed a bit. "All right. Give us everything you've got on Ustadh and whatever you know about this financier, so we know who we're looking for.

Anything you can give us on the meeting site — these Tawila Cisterns — would be appreciated as well."

"I can do that," Upton said. "I've got it all right here."

* * *

Somewhere in Yemen — Now...

"Ryan, think about this," Upton said, his voice rising.

Cross stared at the gun on the coffee table for a long moment. If he leaned forward against the ropes around his legs, he could just reach the weapon with his right hand. Instead, he reached across his body and used his bound left hand to scratch a powerful itch in his right forearm.

"Indeed, think about it," said the nightmare named Ustadh. "You could live a hero or die a self-righteous fool."

"Killing a beaten-up man just so I can live doesn't sound very heroic," Cross said. "Besides, how do I know you won't just kill me anyway when I shoot him?"

"What do you mean 'when'?" Upton chirped.

Cross ignored Upton. "And am I really supposed to believe you'd give me a chance to shoot you instead of him?" Cross continued.

"This is a test of honor," Ustadh said. He spread his hands out as if inviting Cross to shoot him. "Mine no less than yours."

"I can't help but notice that I get shot either way," Upton pointed out.

"You have no honor!" Ustadh snapped at him. "You're a monster! Monsters deserve to die!"

Upton flinched and pressed back against the couch. Ustadh closed his eyes and took a deep, calming breath.

"What's this now?" Cross asked, raising a sore eyebrow. "How is Upton more of a monster than you are?"

"I am just a technician," Ustadh replied. "I make devices and teach the making of such devices. What others do with those devices is not my concern. I make no secret of what my devices are capable of, but they choose to use them anyway. Those others' choices do not make me a monster."

It was as flawed an argument as Cross had ever heard, but he wasn't in a position to debate morality at the moment. "But Upton is a monster?" Cross asked.

"Oh, my," Ustadh said, genuinely surprised. "Do you know what this man does?"

"He hunts terrorists," Cross said.

"Yes," Ustadh said. "And when he finds one, he tells someone like you. And someone like you targets your robotic drones or your cruise missiles at the terrorist. And your missiles fly or your bombs fall. And innocent people die."

"That's warfare, Professor," Upton growled. "If you don't like it then stay out of the business."

"It would be warfare," Ustadh said, "if your enemies were the only ones who died." He spoke slowly, biting off every word in an attempt to keep his anger in check. Cross saw Ustadh's fingers curl into fists as if he were going to lash out and crack Upton across the face.

"But that is not how you operate," Ustadh said. "You don't care who dies when your missiles fly and your bombs fall. You don't care whether innocents die — wives, even children! You don't care as long as your targets perish with them. Do you?"

Upton looked Ustadh in the eye for a second, as if searching for some clever response. But no words passed his lips. He looked away, bringing a triumphant smile to Ustadh's face.

"What are you trying to say?" Cross asked. "Are you telling me he's knowingly called down drone strikes on civilian targets?"

"That is exactly what I'm saying," Ustadh said. "He did it in Iraq many times. He has even committed this same crime here in Yemen, no doubt."

"I have plenty of doubt," Cross said. "Where's your proof?"

"It's true," Upton said. "Not the Yemen bit, but everything else. I've targeted civilian centers where scumbag terrorists were hiding. But those scumbags are the ones putting the civilians in danger, not me. They're taking their own people hostage, thinking they don't have to face justice for their crimes. Well, they're wrong and I've been proving it to them. I've been showing them their actions have consequences. I've been letting them know they can't hide forever."

"He even admits it," Ustadh said. He turned to Cross.

"From his own lips, he names himself a war criminal. His tone makes him sound proud of his actions. Is such a man truly worthy of the breath God gave him?"

"That was quite an admission," Cross said slowly.

"You see why he must die," Ustadh said. "It is your duty."

"And then what?" Cross asked. "What's to stop someone else just as bad from doing what Upton's done...or worse?"

"You are," Ustadh said, his eyes wide. "Take the gun. Shoot him. Show the others that actions have consequences. Let them know they can't hide forever."

* * *

Two Days Before, in Aden, Yemen...

Upton's early reconnaissance footage made the Tawila Cisterns out to be often empty and rarely visited. But on the day of Ustadh's meeting with the AQAP financier, the place was packed. A French tour group had chosen to visit the cisterns that day. They snapped photos with their cell phones and loitered all over the grounds. Their presence (and the handful of locals in attendance) made it easier for Cross and his team to blend into the scenery without drawing attention. However, the idea of something going wrong and gunfire breaking out made Cross feel sick to his stomach. Precautions would need to be taken to protect the civilians.

Thankfully, Lancaster was in the team's armored van down in the parking lot with Chief Walker and Agent Upton. She was keeping an eye on things via Four-Eyes, the small recon and surveillance UAV quad-copter. "I see Ustadh," Lancaster said through Cross's canalphone. "He's just coming in now. Blue thawb, red-and-white cap."

The Cisterns of Tawila's original purpose was to collect and store rainwater runoff from the mountains and to protect the city below them from flooding. However, construction farther upstream had redirected water flow so that the cisterns were no longer necessary. The only use the site had now was as a tourist attraction.

Cross acknowledged Lancaster's report by tapping his canalphone twice. He looked toward the attraction's entrance and idly scratched his right arm. Ustadh was the only one coming in at the moment. He paused to chat in a friendly fashion with the young woman taking admission tickets at the front gate.

Cross and Hospital Corpsman Second Class Kyle Williams were at the lowest level of the cisterns, spread out among a handful of areas, keeping eyes in all directions. After Lancaster's signal, they'd melted into the afternoon shadows to watch Ustadh unobserved.

All the members of the team wore civilian clothes and were armed only with silenced SIG P226 pistols. Beneath their clothes they wore ultralight spider silk and carbon-fiber ballistic vests, which fit as closely as a shirt but could stop small arms and light rifle fire. The only exception was Yamashita on overwatch. The sniper had arrived the previous night after the cisterns had closed down, then climbed high into the surrounding cliffs with his M110 sniper rifle. The hiding spot he'd chosen gave him line of sight on the entire complex, including the parking lot below.

Ustadh drifted up past the first level of the cisterns to the second. "I see him," Yamashita reported.

"He's coming your way, Paxton," Cross murmured via his canalphone.

"Sir," Paxton replied just as quietly from the middle level where he and Shepherd were keeping watch.

The pair of them were playing the part of Western tourists, chattering about what they were looking at and filming everything in sight with their cellphones. Their level was the most crowded by the French-speakers in the tour group, so they were forced to circulate and change positions constantly.

When Ustadh paused briefly on one of the ancient bridges to look down toward the city far below, Shepherd had to hand over his camera and ask a couple of female tourists to take his picture in order to get into a spot within earshot of Ustadh. Shepherd flirted with the tourists in awful French while they giggled and snapped photos of him. The intent was to keep his cover, but he seemed to be enjoying himself.

The target paused on that level for a few minutes then resumed his climb alone. He drew a cigarette and matches from a shiny metal case. Then he climbed to the highest open level of the cisterns. At the top, he lit a cigarette.

"I see him," Jannati said from the top level when Ustadh arrived. Jannati was perched on a bench in the shade and pretending to read a book. A half-empty bottle of water was on the ground beside him. Ustadh took no notice of him.

"I think he just signaled somebody from the stairway," Yamashita said. "This could be it."

"I didn't see a signal," Lancaster said.

"He was turning his mirrored cigarette case in the sun, reflecting it back down the steps," Yamashita said.

Cross paused near the stairway. "Is anybody with him?" Cross murmured.

Jannati double-tapped his canalphone, paused, then did it again. *Negative.*

"Possible contact," Yamashita said. "On the stairway."

"Got him," Lancaster confirmed. "He came in with that big group at two o'clock. Straw hat, cargo shorts. Can't see his face yet."

"Get Four-Eyes down in position where you can," Cross said. "We'll need a shot for Upton."

"I'm trying, sir," Lancaster said, "but something's wrong with Four-Eyes. It's not respond —"

A thundering roar shook the Tawila Cisterns. Adrenaline whip-cracked through Cross's system. His hand was already going for his pistol before he fully realized what was going on. The tourists in his field of vision were frozen in place, though only for the moment.

"Parking lot!" Yamashita said. "IED! IED!" His voice sounded far away in Cross's ringing ears.

Cross spun and took a few steps back in that direction just in time to see a plume of black smoke rising from below. Through a bloom of dust and smoke, he could just make out a scorched, blackened ruin where the French tourists' bus had been. The next nearest vehicle to it, Shadow Squadron's van, lay on its side, leaking fluid. The vehicle's unique armor and construction had kept it from being blown apart, but it had been parked right next to the bus. Were Lancaster, Walker, and Upton still alive? Could they have survived that?

Instead of an answer, chaos came Cross's way. The girl who'd been taking admissions at the foot of the stairway saw the bus. Her scream awoke animal-like terror in the onlookers.

"They're trying to kill us!" someone shouted.

"Go upstairs!" another person cried.

"There could be more bombs! There's never just one!"

"Go down!"

"Get out of the way!"

"Walker!" Cross shouted over the din, battering at his canalphone. "Lancaster! Report!"

"Where's Ustadh?" Yamashita's voice called.

"He was right here!" Jannati answered then let out a loud curse. "I lost him. What's happening down there?"

Cross wished he knew. With the floodgates of panic open, every visitor to the cisterns had suddenly tried to pour down the stairs from the middle level. The lower level was completely jammed. The crowd couldn't decide which way to stampede, so Cross was forced to maintain his position amidst the bubbling cauldron of frightened humanity.

"He's not here!" Jannati cried. "Did he go back down?"

"Man down," Shepherd said, his voice heavy and oddly slurred. "Me. I am that man. Medic?"

"He's all right," Paxton said. "Crowd knocked him into one of the canals. He'll be fine."

"I'm coming," Williams said. Cross saw the medic shoving his way through the people jammed on the lower-level stairwell.

"Belay that," Cross said. "Get to the van. We could have three —"

Cross never saw what stung him. He'd been fighting his way out of the fear-maddened crowd, trying to catch some glimpse of Ustadh when a wasp-like sting jabbed him in the shoulder. His eyes drooped like heavy stage curtains, and he realized he was collapsing.

Did I get a shot, he wondered. He struggled to focus on something in the haze that clouded his sight. *I already had an injection,* he thought deliriously. *Shots suck.*

Cross's mind and body floated in disconnected little bubbles, neither one troubling the other. He felt someone standing over him.

Cross tried to crane his neck to look up, but he couldn't. The person dug the canalphone out of Cross's ear and crushed it under his feet.

"Hey, those are expensive," Cross mumbled.

Someone else knelt on the other side of Cross. The two of them reached out and hefted Cross between them. They shouted in French that their friend needed help and for everyone to clear the way.

The Chief speaks French, too, Cross remembered. The Chief is awesome. *I hope he's okay. Doesn't he have kids...?*

* * *

Baqubah, Iraq. Several Years Ago...

It grew harder to think of the prisoner as an insurgent the longer Lieutenant Cross sat across the table from him. The more the two of them faced each other, the more Cross thought of him as the boy's father.

Cross's SEAL team had captured the man and his seventeen-year-old son at the end of a raid on an Al-Qaeda weapons depot that morning. The boy had been shot in the shoulder as he hung out a window firing an AK-47 wildly with one hand. Cross was the one who'd shot him. Cross had also been the first one into the room where the boy lay after his team had taken the depot. There he'd found the boy's father trying to bandage the wound. The man had looked at a pistol lying nearby when Cross's SEALs entered, but he'd been outnumbered and outgunned. The fight had left him.

And now here the man was, glaring at Cross and refusing to even speak to him except to demand to see his son.

"Your son's being treated," Cross told him again. "As soon as you tell us what we need to know, you'll be reunited. All we want is your cell's supplier. We need to know how you're getting your weapons and who's paying for them."

"Allah provides," the man said sarcastically, his voice dripping with contempt. "We pray and the weapons rain down from Heaven. Every Muslim can do this. Did you not know?"

Cross gritted his teeth. He'd been interrogating the man for hours, and he'd gotten nowhere. His SEAL team had been tasked with breaking up the flow of weapons into the hands of Al-Qaeda militants operating in Iraq, and discovering this depot had been a major find. Yet for all his efforts, Cross had no new information. He was at his wits' end, and the man across the table from him clearly knew it.

Cross took a deep breath and tried talking again. "Listen, I don't want to do this all night. If I let you see your son first, would that get you to —"

Before he could finish the sentence, the door behind him banged open. A man Cross had never met came in. He was white and approaching early middle age, a pair of expensive specs perched on the end of his nose.

"You're Cross?" the newcomer asked. "I'm Bradley Upton, CIA."

"Agent Upton, it's good to finally meet in person," Cross

said. "I take it you're here to take over the interrogation. I haven't been having much luck."

Upton ran a cold, calculating look over Cross, then directed it at the insurgent. "You're Mustafa's father?" Upton asked. He gave Cross a quick glance to tell him to back off. Cross did. "I don't know how to tell you this…"

"He's dead?" the man growled. He tensed in his chair, as if preparing to pounce. Cross put his hand on his pistol.

"He isn't dead," Upton said then let out a sigh. "Not yet. His shoulder is badly infected, though. He's feverish. He's dying. Maybe not today, maybe not tomorrow, but it doesn't look good."

"But I…I bandaged it," the man said. "I cleaned it. I removed the bullet."

"Yeah, you did," Upton said. "But you're not exactly a doctor, are you?"

The boy's father — the man who'd shown Cross nothing but angry defiance all day long — sagged uncertainly in his chair. "I thought I helped him. I tried to take care of him."

"I know," Upton said. "I'm sure you did everything that you could."

"He's going to die? He'll die?" the man asked.

"Well," Upton said, "he certainly could die. Ryan's corpsman has been working on him all night, but there's only so much he can do. The infection is beyond his power to treat."

It took Cross a moment to realize the agent was referring to Pritchard, the corpsman for Cross's SEAL team. The agent had used Cross's first name so casually that Cross hadn't even noticed. He said it like the two of them were old friends or something. Cross assumed Upton had done that to include him in the rapport he was trying to build with the insurgent, but he wished Upton had at least run it by him first.

Regardless, it was the base's surgeons and doctors who'd been treating this man's son, not Cross's medic. *What game is Upton playing?* Cross wondered.

"Is there someone else?" the insurgent asked, his voice thin and distant. "Another doctor?" His eyes had glazed slightly, and he couldn't bring himself to look Upton or Cross in the face anymore.

"There's no time," Upton told him. "Mustafa is dying, and we're a little bit outside the Green Zone. The only hope for him now is to let Ryan's corpsman take off your son's arm."

The insurgent paled. He looked like someone had punched him in the stomach. "Oh, no..."

"Problem is," Upton continued, "he won't let us. We can't get near him with the anesthetics to put him under and do the job. We need your help. You have to convince him that there's no other way to save his life. Can you do that? Will he still listen to you?"

The man nodded slowly. "He always does what I tell him. Eventually. Mustafa. Mustafa..."

The man tried to stand, but Upton held out a hand to stop him. "Wait, where do you think you're going?"

"To my son," the insurgent said, confusion on his face. "But you said —"

"Well, you can't go yet," Upton said. "Isn't there something you're forgetting?"

The man looked at Upton then over at Cross. He was no less confused than a moment ago. "Forgetting what?"

"Ryan here asked you some questions earlier," Upton said. "Don't you think you'd better answer them?"

Upton put his fists on the tabletop that lay between himself and the insurgent. He leaned down to loom over the man. "I sure think you should answer them." His voice was still completely calm, but his eyes blazed with intensity. Cross's breath caught in his throat, and he wasn't even the one Upton was pressuring.

The insurgent tried to reignite his anger, but he couldn't do it. His words died in his throat, and he slumped, defeated, into his chair. "What do you want to know?" he asked.

This time, when Cross asked questions, the man answered quickly and with no trace of defiance. His face burned with shame, but the insurgent told everything he knew about his cell's operation and its connection to Al-Qaeda in Iraq.

It wasn't much, but it was a step in the right direction. It supported certain intelligence Upton and Cross had uncovered separately from other sources and suggested a next target for

Cross's SEAL team. The man told them everything they asked for and more, and did so in a great rush so that he could try to save his dying son.

When the interview was complete, Upton thanked him sincerely, shook his hand, and wished him luck with his son. The agent then motioned for Cross to join him and crossed the room to leave.

"What about me?" the insurgent asked desperately. "When can I see Mustafa?"

"I have to let my superiors know that you cooperated," Upton said. "They'll send a car over for you in five minutes."

"Thank you," the man said. His eyes welled up on the verge of tears. "Oh, thank you. Thank you."

Upton pulled Cross out into the hallway and closed the door on the man. The two of them walked toward the stairwell at the end of the hall. Through the thick stone walls of the building, they could hear the faint booms of artillery shells going off in the city beyond.

"His son's not with my corpsman," Cross said.

"I know," Upton said. He smiled but it didn't wrinkle his eyes the way a real smile would. "I made up that stuff about the kid's arm. Sure turned the dad into a helpful fella, though, didn't it?"

"So he's not really going to lose his arm?" Cross asked.

"Don't see why he should," Upton shrugged. "The kid was barely grazed by the bullet."

Cross flinched. "What?"

"I lied," Upton said flatly. "Whoever shot him barely hit him. Kid was never in any real danger."

"What are you going to do with his father?" Cross blurted out. "He thinks he's going to see his son. I'm guessing that won't happen."

Upton nodded. "Where he's actually going is to the airfield to catch a flight to Guantanamo Bay. Don't worry about it. My people will take care of it. I've got something bigger in mind for the two of us."

Cross's head started to spin. What Upton had done was the cruelest thing he'd ever seen words do to a man, even if it had been undeniably effective. Still, Cross wondered what kind of man could twist a despairing father's heart without even batting an eyelash?

"Interested, Ryan?" Upton said. "If your team's up for it, I can use what he gave us in there to put an op together that'll break Al-Qaeda's supply chain into a thousand pieces. I can even see there's a promotion in it for you if all goes well. That's worth a little white lie between enemies, right?"

"Maybe," Cross murmured, unable to find a reason to believe otherwise. "It was a dirty trick, but it got the job done."

"Good thing we're at war," Upton said with a wink. "Come on. Let's introduce me to your team. We've got work to do yet."

Cross frowned.

* * *

Now, Somewhere in Yemen...

"Ryan, say something," Upton urged. It was alarming to hear panic in the voice of a man who always seemed so in control of himself and the situation.

"Yes," Ustadh said, cocking his head and watching Cross intently. "Say something. Or, better yet, *do* something. What is your decision? Will you kill this man?"

"I'm thinking," Cross said slowly, reaching his free right arm to take the pistol off the table. He rested it on his lap and looked at it.

Upton whimpered. "Ryan..."

"I'm thinking," Cross said, looking up, "that this whole situation feels...staged."

Ustadh's eyes narrowed ever so slightly. That little tell confirmed Cross's suspicions.

"I mean, it's awfully operatic, isn't it, this little stage you've set? And then there's this little dilemma of choosing who lives and who dies." Cross locked eyes with Ustadh. "This obvious irony of a terrorist forcing one American to kill another to punish him for heartless terrorist acts against civilian victims. It's not even operatic. It's melodramatic."

"Don't toy with me," Ustadh said.

Without a word, Cross pointed the pistol at the ceiling and pulled the trigger, looking Ustadh in the eye as he did it.

The gun didn't fire. "Bang," Cross said.

Ustadh turned to Upton. "You were right," Ustadh said.

Upton sat up straight on the sofa and smirked at Cross. "I told him you'd see right through it," he said. "That's 5000 rials you owe me, Ustadh."

Amusement colored Ustadh's face, erasing all trace of the self-righteous terrorist he'd been pretending to be. He shrugged then folded his arms across his chest.

"All right, give us the room," Upton said. "One test is as good as another, I suppose."

Ustadh nodded. He left, closing the door behind him. Upton wriggled and twisted his wrists, loosening the bonds that held his hands together. Once the coils fell slack and dropped on the floor, Upton reached up to his face. He pulled off a layer of latex and fake blood that had made his face look as bruised and abused as Cross's felt.

When Upton was finished, he looked no different than the last time Cross had seen him.

"Sorry I can't do the same for you, Ryan," Upton said.

"That was some test," Cross said. "I assume I passed?"

"You've always shown the cleverness I desire in a soldier," Upton said. "The real issue I wanted to explore was your loyalty. I wanted to know if you could put our friendship in front of the high-minded ideals you military types get drilled into you."

"Friendship?" Cross spat. "Are we friends?"

Upton grinned. "As much as people like us can be, I suppose. You help me get the work done and don't give me a hard time about how I do it. That's rare these days."

"And Ustadh? Is he one of your friends too?"

"He's more like an employee. I saved his life in Baqubah back in 2006 by helping him escape Al-Zarqawi. He's been my little puppy dog ever since."

"And if I'd tried to shoot him?"

"Well, then I would've known for sure you were the man I wanted. As it stands now, however, I've got to figure things out another way." Upton hesitated. "It seems to me you're a straightforward kind of guy. Why don't I just lay it on the table and see what happens?"

"Go ahead," Cross said, struggling to bite back the rage that burned in his chest.

"I'm putting a team together," Upton said. "Top-tier special operators. Smart, capable men who know the value of loyalty but aren't opposed to being handsomely paid for the hard work they do."

"You're trying to rebuild your Special Operations Group?" Cross asked.

"Oh, no. This is a personal operation. All off the record, under the table, answering only to me. This isn't anything the JSOC or the CIA — or anybody else, really — needs to know about. I don't offer health and dental or a retirement package, but the work pays so well you'll never have to worry about any of that stuff."

"What is the work, exactly?" Cross asked.

"It's all about controlling the chaos here in the Middle East," Upton explained. "We keep right on fighting our little war on terror, just like we have been doing, but more with the mindset of a gardener instead of an exterminator. We keep out the dangerous invasive species — the ultra-radicals and the extremists — but tend and nourish the less dangerous plant life. We keep nukes and bio-weapons out of the bad guys' hands, sure, but maybe we turn a blind eye if a rebel group gets its hands on a shipment of rifles or C4. We keep them in check so they don't run rampant, but we don't stomp them out altogether. Not unless they turn their eyes toward America, that is. If they do that, we burn them down and replant."

"I don't see where the money comes from," Cross said. Keeping his voice calm was no easy feat. What Upton was saying made Cross want to vomit.

"Congress," Upton said. "Those guys pay through the nose in foreign aid money to keep terrorist threats bottled up in faraway countries like this one. If a foreign government calls itself a US ally in the war on terror and looks like it's trying hard to fight Al-Qaeda, our government practically throws money at it to help the cause. Not every regime knows how to take advantage of that system, though."

"But you do," Cross said.

Upton nodded. "And for a modest percentage, I can inform certain friends I've made in regimes around the region. I show them how the game is played, then I — we — help them tend their gardens."

"You did this in Iraq?" Cross asked.

"Iraq put my kids through college," Upton said. "Ivy League, even."

"Yemen too?" Cross asked.

"Yemen is where you come in," Upton said. "You and anyone else I can get for the team. Al-Qaeda's in bloom here, but we're going to have to work quickly before any other, um...*gardeners* get ahead of us."

"You seem awfully sure I'm already in," Cross said. "I turned you down the last time you tried to recruit me, remember? I joined Shadow Squadron instead."

Upton waved dismissively. "That wasn't a choice. The general put you on the spot at the end of your last tour of duty. I have no doubt whatsoever that if you'd turned him down then he would've found some other pretext to pull you back into the Navy for another four years no matter what I had to say about it."

"Probably," Cross admitted.

"And it's not like I'm trying to make you into one of the bad guys. There are real threats out there that need to be knocked down, and I want you in charge of prioritizing them and taking them out. You can be involved in the other side or the money part as much or as little as you want."

"I'd be lying if I said I wasn't tempted," Cross lied. "But I don't think you're giving me much more of a choice than the general did."

"Worse, actually," Upton confirmed. "But I've got a good read on you, Ryan. One thing you've never been is stupid. You came into the Navy with high ideals, but you've seen how the real world works now. You've seen how evil prospers no matter what so-called 'good men' do about it. You've seen how our government keeps making the same mistakes over and over again, and the world keeps on spiraling out of control. Right now, you're powerless in the face of all that, but I can offer you a better life. With me, you can make a difference. And you can make an obscene amount of money."

Cross grunted. "But if I say no —"

"Then the cover story about what happened to you becomes true," Upton declared. "Right now, your team knows that you and I were kidnapped during a terrorist attack at the Tawila Cisterns. For all they know, extremists murdered us. In a few days, they're going to find two bodies that confirm their suspicions. If you turn me down now, only one of those bodies is going to be a fake. And I assure you that this is not melodrama. I like you, Ryan, but I will kill you rather than let you become a liability."

Cross took a deep breath. "I thought I knew you pretty well, Bradley. Up until a few weeks ago, I figured you were just a smug, cynical, self-centered charmer. All the same, I always figured that at least you were on our side. But Command was right about you all along."

A tiny crease appeared over Upton's eyes. "Command? What are you talking about?"

"They know," Cross said. "This scam you're so proud of. The one you were running in Iraq. The one you're trying to get started here in Yemen. They know all about it. You've done a brilliant job of hiding it, but this is the twenty-first century. You've laundered money and squirreled it away in offshore accounts and Swiss banks and fake investments. But as good as you are, we've got people who are better. They figured you out, and now you've played right into their hands."

In truth, Command hadn't foreseen that Upton would use the Yemen operation as an attempt to recruit Cross to his criminal enterprise. *But Upton doesn't need to know that,* Cross thought.

"Originally we were just looking for an opportunity to snatch you up without disrupting CIA operations all across Yemen," Cross went on. "But when you offered up Ustadh, I admit I got greedy. He made for very good bait. All the same, things have worked out so far. Here you are, and here I am."

For the first time in as long as Cross had known him, a genuine smile came to Upton's face. Mirth lit his eyes and he let out a snort. The snort turned into a chuckle. Then the floodgates opened and Upton burst into a teary-eyed guffaw.

"You. Are. Priceless!" Upton wheezed, struggling to get

himself under control. "This is a sting? This? Well then I guess I surrender! Should I untie you now so you can take me into custody. Or would you like to hit me with that empty gun a few times first?"

Cross smiled back, though it was a sad, pitying one. "Let me show you something..."

Without waiting for a reply, Cross used his bound left hand to unbutton his right sleeve's cuff and pulled the sleeve up to his elbow. On the inside of his right forearm was an itchy red welt that had been bothering Cross all week. He turned his arm so Upton could see the mark.

"Command needed to be able to find me in case you got me away from my team," Cross said. "So before we left, our doctor injected a subcutaneous GPS transponder under my skin. Wherever it is you've taken me, my team's already found you. They might not get here in time to stop you from killing me, but you're not going to get away."

As the reality of the situation sank in, the smile faded from Upton's face. He reached into his jacket and produced a matte-black .45 caliber M1911 pistol. He stood and aimed the pistol at Cross's head. "Then I suppose we have nothing more to talk about." He frowned then added with real confusion, "How did I read you so wrong?"

As the last word left Upton's mouth, the lights went out, plunging the room into darkness. Reacting on pure instinct, Cross lifted the empty SIG P226 in his right hand and hurled it where Upton's face had been. Fortunately, Upton proved a split second too slow in the darkness.

Cross's pistol smashed Upton in the face, throwing his aim off. The bullet nicked Cross alongside his temple, drawing a line of fire above his ear. He hissed in pain, but he knew Upton had gotten the worst of it. The CIA agent lurched backward and sat down hard on the sofa, dropping his pistol.

"Zahid!" Upton shouted, spitting blood and clutching his nose. "Get in here!" He thumped down off the couch and groped blindly on the floor for his gun.

Whether Zahid was Ustadh's real name or the name of another of Upton's men, Cross didn't know. He heard feet thumping down the hallway outside the door and did the first thing he could think of. With a tremendous heave, he lurched sideways and tipped his chair over onto its right side.

Cross came down hard on his shoulder but managed not to pin his arm under his body. Like Upton, he flailed around in search of the dropped M1911.

With a thunderous crash, the door came off one hinge and swung into the room by the remains of the other hinge.

"Ha!" Upton crowed at the same moment, finding his pistol and aiming it at Cross.

"Drop it!" someone barked in Midwestern-accented English. "Drop it, Upton!" Lancaster ordered.

He didn't. Two shots rang out in quick succession.

Then all was silent.

* * *

Now, in Qulansiyah, Yemen...

Williams dabbed the cut on Cross's temple with something cold and astringent. "Is that where we are?" Cross asked, pointing at Lancaster's touchpad.

"Yes, sir," Lancaster said over Williams' shoulder. "Qulansiyah to be exact. This was Ustadh's safe house, as far as we can tell."

"How are you feeling?" Cross asked. "Last I saw you, you were in the van. When that bus blew up right next to it, I feared the worst."

"I'm fine, sir," Lancaster said. "I got lucky. But the Chief got the worst of it. His hearing's damaged. He might be permanently deaf. We don't know yet. And he's...see, when the van..."

"His back's broken," Williams finished for her. "Barring a miracle, he's going to be paralyzed from the waist down."

The news hit Cross like a punch in the gut. Despite being seated, he felt like he was falling.

"Shepherd has a concussion from his fall at the cisterns," Williams went on. "Jannati and Paxton each took a couple of shots in their vests on the way in here, but they're up and about. I need to check on them again once we're done here. They got the wind knocked out of them pretty bad, but the ballistic vests got the job done."

"You're done here," Cross said softly. "Go take care of the others."

Williams frowned but knew better than to refuse. He gathered up his supplies and left the room, sparing a look at Bradley Upton's blanket-covered body in the corner before he left.

"Doesn't feel like a win, does it?" Cross asked Lancaster when they were the only ones left in the room. He couldn't take his eyes off Upton's still form. Lancaster stared as well. Her bullet had taken his life. Upton's own shot had gone into the wall just beside her.

"Well," she said, "we did stop him. And we even captured Ustadh. That should feel like a win, shouldn't it?"

Cross shrugged. While the others had finished checking the safe house and rounding up the rest of Upton's men, he told Lancaster about what Upton had wanted from him.

When Cross finished speaking, he could tell Lancaster wanted to say something. After a few moments, Lancaster finally worked up the courage. "Did he really think he knew you, sir?"

"What?" Cross asked.

"I mean, I don't think I know you all that well just yet," she continued, "but I wouldn't have expected you to turn traitor just for money. Or for any reason, really." She looked at Upton's body. "Did he honestly think that you would go along with his plan?"

Cross sighed. "Maybe he wanted to prove something to himself. Maybe he thought that if he could convince me to get

on board with this racket of his, then maybe what he was doing wouldn't seem quite as bad to him."

"So what did he want?" Lancaster asked. "Your approval?"

"Could be."

"Why you?"

Cross grunted. "He liked me. I respected him, and I didn't get on his case about how he did his job. He didn't get that a lot. I might have been the closest thing he had to a friend."

"He still tried to kill you."

"Well, I didn't say I was going to miss him," Cross said. He'd meant it to be a joke, but it hadn't come out that way. Instead it sounded flat, hollow, lifeless. The way he felt.

"Sir, about the Chief…"

"Not now, Lancaster," Cross said. "I'm not ready to have that conversation yet."

Lancaster nodded. "Well, when you're ready, sir," she said, "we're here."

For now, Cross thought. He glanced at Upton's body, wondering where he was going to find the courage to face Chief Walker.

You're all here now, Cross thought. *But for how long?*

The dead man gave him no answers.

MISSION DEBRIEFING

OPERATION

DARK AGENT

5678

MISSION COMPLETE

PRIMARY OBJECTIVES

- Locate the "the Professor"

- Capture him alive

SECONDARY OBJECTIVES

- Maintain covert presence in Yemen

3245.98 ● ● ●

STATUS

3/3 COMPLETE

CROSS, RYAN

RANK: Lieutenant Commander
BRANCH: Navy Seal
PSYCH PROFILE: Team leader
of Shadow Squadron. Control
oriented and loyal, Cross insisted
on hand-picking each member of
his squad.

I keep telling myself it could've been worse. Everyone
made it out alive, we eliminated a terrible bomb maker and
exposed a corrupt CIA agent, and you all managed to save
my skin, but all I can think about right now is the Chief. His
unflinching commitment and military expertise are a vital
part of Shadow Squadron. I don't want to consider the
possibility that we might lose him.

That said, great work out there...and thanks again for
saving my life.

– Lieutenant Commander Ryan Cross

ERROR

UNAUTHORIZED

USER MUST HAVE LEVEL 12 CLEARANCE
OR HIGHER IN ORDER TO GAIN ACCESS
TO FURTHER MISSION INFORMATION.

2019.681

AUTHOR DEBRIEFING

ACCESS GRANTED

CARL BOWEN

Q/When and why did you decide to become a writer?

A/I've enjoyed writing ever since I was in elementary school. I wrote as much as I could, hoping to become the next Lloyd Alexander or Stephen King, but I didn't sell my first story until I was in college. It had been a long wait, but the day I saw my story in print was one of the best days of my life.

Q/What made you decide to write *Shadow Squadron*?

A/As a kid, my heroes were always brave knights or noble loners who fought because it was their duty, not for fame or glory. I think the special ops soldiers of the US military embody those ideals. Their jobs are difficult and often thankless, so I wanted to show how cool their jobs are, but also express my gratitude for our brave warriors.

Q/What inspires you to write?

A/My biggest inspiration is my family. My wife's love and support lifts me up when this job seems too hard to keep going. My son is another big inspiration.

He's three years old, and I want him to read my books and feel the same way I did when I read my favorite books as a kid. And if he happens to grow up to become an elite soldier in the US military, that would be pretty awesome, too.

Q/Describe what it was like to write these books.
A/The only military experience I have is a year I spent in the Army ROTC. It gave me a great respect for the military and its soldiers, but I quickly realized I would have made a pretty awful soldier. I recently got to test out a friend's arsenal of firearms, including a combat shotgun, an AR-15 rifle, and a Barrett M82 sniper rifle. We got to blow apart an old fax machine.

Q/What is your favorite book, movie, and game?
A/My favorite book of all time is *Don Quixote*. It's crazy and it makes me laugh. My favorite movie is either *Casablanca* or *Double Indemnity*, old black-and-white movies made before I was born. My favorite game, hands down, is *Skyrim*, in which you play a heroic dragonslayer. But not even *Skyrim* can keep me from writing more *Shadow Squadron* stories, so you won't have to wait long to read more about Ryan Cross and his team. That's a promise.

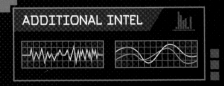

ADDITIONAL INTEL

ARTIST

WILSON TORTOSA

Wilson "Wunan" Tortosa is a Filipino comic book artist best known for his works on *Tomb Raider* and the American relaunch of *Battle of the Planets* for Top Cow Productions. Wilson attended Philippine Cultural High School, then went on to the University of Santo Tomas, where he graduated with a Bachelor's Degree in Fine Arts, majoring in Advertising.

COLORIST

BENNY FUENTES

Benny Fuentes lives in Villahermosa, Tabasco, in Mexico, where the temperature is just as hot as the sauce. He studied graphic design in college, but now he works as a full-time colorist in the comic book and graphic novel industry for companies like Marvel, DC Comics, and Top Cow Productions. He shares his home with two crazy cats, Chelo and Kitty, who act like they own the place.

3245.98 ● ● ●

2012.101

SIGNING OFF